COLTER SONS BOOK 1

THE RELUCTANT CATTLEMAN

Karen Baney

desert life
media

The Reluctant Cattleman: Colter Sons Book 1
By Karen Baney

Publisher:
Desert Life Media, LLC
Gilbert, AZ 85295

www.karenbaney.com

Printed in the United States of America

ISBN-979-8-9858202-7-0

And whatever you do, in word or deed, do everything in the name of the Lord Jesus, giving thanks to God the Father through him.

–Colossians 3:17

CHAPTER 1

My name is Sam Colter. Samuel when Mama is about to take me to task, which is hardly ever.

I am the second to oldest of the Colter sons and I am the misfit. None of my brothers are like me. James, the oldest, wants to conquer the world with a new enterprise he has yet to discover. He's two weeks shy of being an entire year older than me. James should be the one to take over the ranch, but he's far too ambitious to be tied down. It's just a matter of time before Papa realizes that me, the steady, predictable, and dependable one, will be the son that runs the place one day.

Boone is the third son, the wildest of us all. His barometer for risk is broken. Old Grandpa Ben, he wasn't really our grandpa, but that's what we called him, used to say that Boone was just too stupid to know he was in trouble, or he was some darned fool.

Then there's Deacon, the fourth son. By the time he came along, Mama wondered if she had done something wrong to get saddled with four boys under the age of six. Deacon was the most resourceful of us all. He could build a fort with sticks, hay, and rope.

Then there was the baby, Preston. He was quiet, like me, but only on the outside. Inside of that kid, there was some storm a raging. Someday it was gonna come out and shoot if I didn't want to be there when it did.

That brings me to my story. Like I said, I'm the misfit. The quiet one. Cautious. Dependable. Anxious as all get out on the inside. Smart. Leastwise, that's what Mama always says. I looked more like a cross between my papa, with my dark hair and my mama with my bright blue eyes.

If you ask anyone in the family who Mama's favorite was, they would all say it was me. None of us knew the reason she favored me until the year I turned twenty-one.

That was the year where one letter from a journalist named E. M. Thatcher changed my life forever.

CHAPTER 2

Colter Ranch, Arizona Territory
May 4, 1887

SAM

I returned from Prescott after a trip to pick up the mail and the ledgers from the butcher shop that my cousin, Eddie Colter, ran with his wife, Annabel. Eddie was roughly eight years older than me, so he was twenty-eight then.

Eddie worked with Daniel Raulings, who we all called Snake, for several years at the ranch to learn to butcher. He also learned how to smoke bacon, brisket, and more. Eddie was ready to take over the butcher shop and meat company when he turned twenty. Snake still butchered and smoked some of the meat out at the ranch, but Eddie ran that business with Annabel's help.

I managed the finances of the meat company, the ranch, and Uncle Adam's horse breeding and training business.

When I arrived back home, I set the mail and the meat company's bills and books on the table. Two of my brothers were still at school. James was off somewhere in northern Arizona with his railroad job, and Boone was apprenticing with a surveyor.

"How are Eddie and Annabel?" Mama asked as she poured me a glass of lemonade.

"Fine. Looks like they'll have a new addition to their family soon."

"Oh, I should make them a blanket."

I thanked her for the lemonade and sat down at the table, sorting through the mail. A letter with a postmark from Chino Valley caught my eye. It was from E. M. Thatcher.

I opened it right as the door flew open.

"Clear the table!" Warren Cahill shouted.

I jumped to my feet and grabbed the stack of mail and books. Mama swiped up my lemonade just before Warren and two of the cowboys brought Papa in and set him on the table.

"What happened?" Mama asked as Papa groaned in pain.

A trail of blood dotted the floor. My eyes searched for the source of the blood. It was Papa's leg. I dropped my things on the desk when I felt woozy. It was where I should have put them, anyway. Sometimes I preferred working at the table because there was more room to spread out. Plus, Mama often sat and chatted with me for a bit.

"He got gouged in the leg by that ornery bull," Warren said.

"I'm sorry, Hannah," Papa said between groans.

Mama walked over to the pantry and pulled out her medical bag. She always had tonics, medicines, and bandages on hand. She took a pair of scissors and cut the leg of Papa's pants so she could get a better look at the wound.

"It's not too deep, but it is going to require stitches. Do you want me to do it? Or I can send for the doctor?"

I already knew what Papa would say before he said it. Mama always cared for any injury or illness on the ranch. Because the ranch was about an hour outside of town, she patched up whatever needed patching long before the doctor arrived.

"You do it," Papa said.

She poured him some whiskey, and he tossed it back. As he laid down on the table, Mama got to work. She always kept a warm pot of water on, so she quickly sterilized a needle.

After that, I couldn't watch without fear of passing out. I didn't want to pass out right before my brothers got home. I'd never live it down.

My stomach churned, so I walked over to the open window and breathed in the fresh late spring air.

"There," Mama said. "Now, get off my table so I can scrub it down before supper."

I glanced over my shoulder and saw the bandaged wound. I helped Papa to the couch after the cowboys left. He laid down.

"Just prop that leg up," Mama said as she handed him some willow bark tea.

His legs were longer than the couch, so he had little choice.

I asked Mama if she needed help, but she shooed me out of the way. I found my lemonade and went over to the desk.

"Will, you're gonna need to stay off that leg until it heals. At least a few days."

Papa frowned. He wasn't one to sit idle. His face looked pale, and he closed his eyes after he finished the tea.

I returned to the mail and remembered the letter from E. M. Thatcher. I opened it and scanned the letter.

"Mama," I said as I heard her scrubbing the table and then the floor. "Let me read you this letter."

"It is from E. M. Thatcher. He says he's a journalist with

the Prescott Gazette. The earliest pioneers in the area are being interviewed by him. He just published his first article on Grandma Betty and her son, Paul, about his boardinghouse."

Grandma Betty wasn't really our grandma. She was like a mother to Mama, so we treated her like our grandma before she passed.

"Oh?"

"He included a copy of the article if you'd like to read it."

"Maybe after supper."

"Anyway, he heard from Paul that you were part of the same wagon train and that you might have an interesting story to tell. He wants to come out to the ranch for a few weeks this summer to interview you and Papa."

Mama finished cleaning everything and joined me in the parlor.

"Will, did you hear that?" she asked.

"Yup."

"What do you think?"

"I suppose that'd be fine. He can have James's room. If James comes back, then he can double up with Sam."

I frowned. I wasn't sure if Papa meant E. M. Thatcher or James would be my roommate. Either way, I was already sharing a room with Boone. I definitely did not want a second roommate. I was a man and had responsibilities, unlike my three younger brothers. Besides, I hoped to take over James's room.

"Did he say when he would be here?" Mama asked.

I scanned the letter again. "No. I think he is waiting for an invitation from us before setting some dates."

"Can you write back to him that we would be happy to have him come for a visit at his earliest convenience?" Mama said.

I pulled out a fresh sheet of paper and scrawled a quick reply. "You want me to sign for you, Papa?" I usually did because an accident before I was born left Papa unable to read. It was why I took an active role in the businesses.

"Go ahead. You can mail it when you go to the stock-yards tomorrow."

"Me?" My chest tightened.

I hated the stockyards. Dozens of smelly cattle kicked up dust. They looked mean. Hopefully, Papa would not expect me to know how to pick out the stock he wished to purchase. I spent most of my life avoiding the creatures.

I know. It sounds dumb. Even though I grew up on a ranch, I hated cattle. I worked with them as little as Papa would allow. My forte was numbers. I managed a budget better than anyone else on the ranch. But cattle? No, thank you.

"I need you to go with Warren and George. You'll be my representative since I can't go."

"Can't you send Boone?"

"He has his job and James is still gone. So, it falls to you."

I bowed my head and let my shoulders slump forward. I really hated the stockyards.

At least I was a decent rider and wouldn't embarrass my-self riding into town with Warren Cahill and George Lar-son, the other two co-owners of the ranch. George was about twenty years older than Papa, while Warren was rela-tively close to Papa's age. They were partners for as long as I could remember. If there was ever a disagreement, Papa got the deciding vote, as he had the largest stake in the ranch. He stayed out of the horse business. That was Uncle Adam's alone.

I sighed and returned to sorting through the mail and

paying the bills. It was more interesting than dwelling on the trip to the stockyards.

The next morning, I donned my only pair of denim pants and a cotton button-down shirt. Most of my clothes were nice suits, which I preferred over the getup I had to wear to the stockyards.

Papa did not join us for breakfast that morning. He wasn't feeling too well from his encounter with that bull. I ate quickly and headed out to the barn to saddle my horse.

When I arrived at the barn, Aunt Julia finished saddling up her horse. She tied her long brown curly hair back with a ribbon. She wore her cowgirl hat and split skirt. I figured she was gonna help us bring back whatever cattle we purchased.

After I saddled my pinto gelding, Bailey, I joined Aunt Julia, Warren, and Georgie.

"Where's George?" I asked.

"He's sick, so he asked me to take care of things," Georgie said. Georgie was George's oldest son and my aunt Julia's brother-in-law. Looked like we had plenty of representation from the Larson clan.

Two of the cowboys joined us. I was grateful for it. Hope-fully, I wouldn't have to do much of anything besides pay for the stock.

An hour later, the six of us arrived at the stockyards north of Prescott. I excused myself to mail the letter to E. M. Thatcher before I returned to the stockyards. When I got back, Warren examined several heifers and bulls. Their plan was to buy a new bull to replace the ornery sucker that gouged Papa's leg yesterday.

"You look like a real cattleman," Aunt Julia teased me as she propped a leg on the rail of the corral and pulled my cowboy hat a little lower on my head.

I pushed my hat back up to where I liked it. "I grew up on a ranch."

"Yeah, most days it doesn't seem like it. You think you could run the place if anything were to happen to Will?"

My stomach tightened, and my throat constricted. "Nothing is gonna happen to Papa."

"Not now. But someday he's gonna want to stop working so hard."

Warren and Georgie waved me over. Aunt Julia followed beside me.

"I think this bull is the best choice," Warren said.

Aunt Julia entered the pen to look the creature over. I stayed outside of it. She always had been fearless.

"I think he's sound," she said when she stepped out of the pen.

When they asked my opinion, my tongue tied up in knots. I think I managed an intelligent answer, since none of them looked at me like I was crazy. The three of them selected five heifers in all.

I paid the stockyard owner and joined them on my horse. Then we drove the cattle the back way to the ranch. When I say we, I really mean everyone but me. I kept Bailey near enough to the back of the cattle but contributed little in the way of help.

I never did like the back way to the ranch. Something about coming to the ranch from the northwest never felt right. It was more than that. I got downright anxious, sweaty palms, sweaty neck, shallow breaths. It just unsettled me in a way that made no rational sense.

When we drove the cattle down into the valley, I parted ways with everyone else. Julia, Warren, and Georgie drove the bull into the pen by the barn while the cowboys took the heifers out with the rest of the herd. I took Bailey into the barn and brushed him down, glad to be home.

As soon as I was done, I changed back into my normal clothes and set about my normal job.

CHAPTER 3

Prescott, Arizona Territory
June 1, 1887

ELLIE MAE

As my papa pulled the wagon to a stop in front of Lancaster's Boardinghouse, I smiled. I was finally ready to start my new job at the Prescott Gazette. The editor published my first few articles in the Prescott Pioneers series. Prescott was founded twenty-three years ago. The series featured current residents who were some of the earliest settlers. I told their stories about the early days, using my pen name E. M. Thatcher.

I conducted the first interview with Paul Lancaster back in March, when Papa was in town on business. They had been friends for several years. Whenever Papa came to Prescott from our home in Chino Valley, he stayed at Paul's boardinghouse.

Before the end of that trip, I submitted two articles to the Prescott Gazette. The first was about Paul Lancaster and his late mother. They were on the wagon train with the first governor, and they came from the Midwest to start a boardinghouse. The second story was about the Osborn family and their restaurant. The editor published both stories. He asked me to move to the area to write a weekly article for the series.

Paul unloaded my Remington 2 typewriter from the wagon and carried it into his barn at the boardinghouse. He treated the machine with great care. It was a gift from Papa to start my new career. Papa draped a canvas tarp over it.

My heart squeezed a little to leave the machine in a barn. Until I met with the Colter family and settled in at their ranch, it made little sense to cart the heavy machine around.

Papa kissed my cheek and said his farewells so he could make it back home before dark, but not before extracting a promise from Paul and his wife, Millie, that they would check on me from time to time.

I headed over to the livery that Paul suggested. It was owned by a man named Thomas Anderson. I rented a gentle mare with a sidesaddle. Then I secured my satchel and valise behind the saddle. Thomas gave me directions to the ranch and a boost up to the saddle. Then I pointed the mare out of town.

The sun warmed my back. My straw hat shaded my face. I wore a simple brown skirt and a white long-sleeved shirt-waist, which protected my fair skin from the intensity of the sun. The air was fresh, but warm as it was shortly after noon.

My stomach growled, and I scolded myself for not eating before I left town. I was too eager to get to the ranch as early in the day as possible. I could hardly wait to interview Hannah Colter. Her insight would help me tell a more compelling story about the founding of Prescott.

It had been a while since I rode, so I kicked the mare into a gallop. The wind against my face brought warmth to my cheeks. I didn't slow the mare down until I crested the top of the last hill before the ranch appeared in the valley below. It was significantly bigger than I imagined.

For as far as my eyes could see, there were buildings. All the way from the other side of a lake to the horizon stretched a magnificent herd of cattle. There was a corral near the barn where two people worked with a very green horse that kept rearing up on its hind legs. I was a little worried for them, having never seen such an antsy horse before. Within minutes, it seemed they had the animal under control.

A fast rider whizzed past me and down into the valley. He did not stop until he was in front of the yellow house with white trim. From the distance, I could not discern much about him other than he dismounted and headed into the house.

As I pointed the mare toward the yellow house, another young man, and a woman, likely his mother, stepped onto the porch. I took a deep breath and let it out slowly.

It was deceitful to let them think that E. M. Thatcher was a man. When I wrote to potential sources as a woman, they did not return my correspondence. I learned over the past few months that people were more willing to let me stay and inter-view them, despite the deception. If no one gave me the time of day, I could not hardly be a journalist.

So, yes, I had written to the Colter family generically, keeping my gender obscured. I knew they were friends with Paul Lancaster, so I also emphasized that connection. The day I received the letter back from Will Colter, I nearly danced all the way home from the post office. I was welcome for some length of time, which meant I could pry both Will and Hannah for information about their experiences, as well as some of the other family that lived on the ranch. If all went as I hoped, I might get some ideas for my novel.

When I reined in the mare near the house, Mrs. Colter was the first to greet me.

"Afternoon!" she said to me. Then she turned to the dark-haired young man next to her. "Sam, help her down."

The redheaded young man frowned. Clearly, he hoped to be chosen for the task.

As Sam came over, I unhooked my leg from the leading pommel and slid toward the back of the saddle as he held the reins. He looped the reins over the porch rail. Then he lifted his hands. After adjusting my skirt so it would not catch on anything, I slid down. His hands grasped my small waist as I rested my hands on his shoulders.

My heart fluttered as I looked into his brilliant blue eyes, more radiant than a cloudless Arizona sky. His hands re-main-ed on my waist, and I quite enjoyed it. I took a quick breath and caught the scent of cedar. Perhaps he stored his clothes in a cedar-lined wardrobe, I wondered.

Still, he didn't release my waist. I didn't push him away.

"Hello, Sam," I said. My voice sounded soft to me.

His gaze did not leave mine. He must be a man with a rich inner voice, one who observed intently and said noth-ing.

How long we stared at each other became awkward. I was in no hurry to move. Neither was he.

"Sam," his mother said. "Why don't you escort our guest inside?"

Finally, words escaped his lips.

"Ma'am." The address sounded natural for him. Some as-pect of it seemed out of place with his nice suit. It was something a cowboy might say, and he definitely did not look like a cowboy.

Then he let go of my waist, offered me his arm, and led

me inside their home. The redheaded young man held the door open, and we walked past him without acknowledging him.

"Would you care for some lemonade?" Mrs. Colter asked.

"Yes, thank you," I said as I dropped my hand from Sam's arm. My breathing finally returned to normal. Right then, my stomach growled loud enough for half the county to hear. Heat warmed my cheeks, and I chastised myself again for not eating lunch.

"I can fix up some sandwiches, too. Boone just got home, and I'm sure he's famished."

I surmised Boone must have been the redhead. He dropped my things on the floor by the door.

"I'll go take care of your horse after I see to mine," Boone said.

Sam held a chair out for me, and I took a seat at the long oak table. Ten ladder-back chairs surrounded the table. I had not asked Paul how many children the Colters had. Judging by the number of chairs, they might have a large family.

"I really appreciate your hospitality, Mrs. Colter."

"Please, call me Hannah."

I thanked her as she set the lemonade in front of me.

"And just who are you?" Sam found his voice.

"Oh, I'm sorry. I am Ellie Mae Thatcher, the journalist. You know, E. M. Thatcher."

All hint of softness left Sam's face as a frown replaced it. I took a deep breath as the news of my identity hung in the air like a thick cloud of smoke.

CHAPTER 4

SAM

"Incoming female rider," Boone announced as he skidded his black stallion, Outlaw, to an abrupt stop in front of me and Mama.

"Are we expecting anyone?" Mama asked.

I shook my head. E. M. Thatcher was the only person we were expecting. Not some woman.

"She looked pretty," Boone said.

"How would you know?" I asked. "You flew past her."

"Trust me, I noticed."

I rolled my eyes. My heart raced a little faster than normal. The only women who visited the ranch were close friends or relatives.

As she came into view, I noticed her sandy colored hair, which was pulled back into a knot just below the base of her straw wide-brimmed hat. I couldn't see her eyes yet, as the shadow of her hat hid them. Her lips were full, which was something I never noticed about anyone. It perplexed me why I might think about it then. Her white blouse hung loosely over her slight frame. Her subtle curves suited her well.

I swallowed hard as she stopped in front of us. Mama

asked me to help her, so I did.

When the stranger put her hands on my shoulders, I held her waist and helped her down. The smile on her lips stole my breath away. Her nutmeg eyes sparkled with life.

As I eased her to the ground, I noticed everything about her. She smelled like the rain after a monsoon storm, sweet and beckoning. Her fair skin looked smooth. The sunlight streaked her sandy hair with honey gold. She was the most gorgeous woman in Arizona.

I liked the way my hands felt against her petite waist. She was shorter than me, but several inches taller than Mama. I wasn't sure how long I stood there holding her. Shoot, she was holding onto my shoulders for just as long, and I really liked it.

Then Mama interrupted my thoughts and asked me to escort her into our home. I did, ignoring the way Boone practically drooled as he held the door open.

Once we were inside, I held a chair out for her. Then I sat across from her. Mama set out a lemonade for each of us.

I sipped mine when the woman finally introduced herself. Thankfully, I swallowed before she finished speaking.

"You're E. M. Thatcher?" I frowned. E. M. Thatcher was supposed to be a man. A man who was going to stay in the room next to mine. I shifted in my chair and ran a finger along the tight collar of my shirt.

"Yes." She sipped the lemonade.

"Oh," Mama said. Then she smiled as if E. M. Thatcher being a woman was nothing at all. "Welcome. We are happy to have you here."

Just then, Papa entered the house. I was certain Boone found him and told him about our woman visitor.

"Will," Mama said. "This is Ellie Mae Thatcher. The journalist."

Papa frowned and directed his statement to me. "I thought the journalist was a man."

The temptation was to close my eyes as I feared I disappointed him yet again. "I can get the letter."

"That misunderstanding is my fault," Ellie Mae said. "I apologize for not being clear in my correspondence. People won't respond if they think I'm a woman journalist, so I made my letter sound like I was a man. I know this is a terrible way to introduce myself."

Mama came around and patted her hand. I tried to keep my jaw from falling open. "I completely understand. Miss Thatcher, it is wonderful that you are making a career out of writing."

"Please, call me Ellie Mae."

Mama nodded and returned to the kitchen to finish making the sandwiches.

Boone burst through the door, which was the only way Boone entered a room. "What did I miss?"

We went through the entire series of introductions again. It chafed at me, especially when Papa frowned my direction. I don't think he believed that the blame for the mistaken identity rested solely on Miss Thatcher.

Mama set some sandwiches in front of Boone and Ellie Mae. My annoyance over the mistaken identity kept me from admitting how much I liked her name and her pretty eyes.

Boone grinned and shoved almost half of a sandwich in his mouth. He was almost nineteen and I would turn twenty-one in a few days. I acted older. Boone? He acted like a wild animal most of the time. He ate with gusto.

I sipped on my lemonade, trying to wipe away the frown from my face.

"Hannah," Papa said. "I think we should fix up Ben's old

place for her."

"Right," Mama nodded. "Sam, see if your cousins, Penny and Dory, can clean up the place."

I stood and walked out of the house with Papa on my heels.

"Sam."

"Papa, you can't be mad at me for this. Her letter didn't hint that she was a… A *she*."

"Whoa. I wasn't saying anything about that. I was going to ask you to watch out for her. Not that I don't trust your brothers, but you know them. I would prefer if you made it your business to know where Ellie Mae is on the property. Don't leave her alone with any of them, especially Boone. We can't afford to have questions about her reputation while she stays on our ranch."

I frowned. It disappointed me that Papa thought he could not trust my brothers. I could not imagine one of them laying a hand on her.

"Look," Papa softened his tone. "Even though there is nothing to worry about from your brothers, I would appreciate you keeping an eye on her. That's all."

"Yes, sir."

Papa headed off toward the barn while I headed over to Aunt Julia's house. I found my cousins outside as they hung the last of the wash on the clothesline.

"Mama sent me over to see if you would clean Grandpa Ben's old place."

"Why?" sixteen-year-old Dory asked.

"We've got a journalist staying with us for a while."

"Can't he just stay in James's room?" Penny asked.

"He's a *she*."

"A woman journalist?" nineteen-year-old Penny's face lit.

"Yup. Can the two of you handle it, or do you need me to send over Preston or Deacon?"

"The place has been vacant for years. Is Boone around? Maybe he can come over and scare off any critters," Penny suggested.

"I'll send him over to help."

As I walked away, I heard the excitement in their chatter. They seemed taken with our female journalist without having met her.

I headed back to the house. When I opened the door, Boone finished his last sandwich.

"The girls want you to scare off any critters," I said to him.

He stood and hurried out the door.

"Can I help with the dishes?" Ellie Mae asked Mama.

"No. It won't take me but a minute to clean up."

Without glancing at Ellie Mae, I walked into the parlor to my desk. I was not in the mood to talk, and my work waited.

A few minutes later, I heard Mama and Ellie Mae talking outside near the clothesline. I looked out the open window and saw Ellie Mae helping Mama while they talked.

She left her hat inside. Her hair glowed in the sunlight, which gave her an angelic quality.

I scolded myself for being so smitten.

As I shuffled the ledgers on my desk, I found the one I was looking for. I studied the numbers but could not concentrate.

"How many children do you have?" Ellie Mae's words floated on the breeze.

"Five boys and one girl. James, the oldest, is somewhere in northern Arizona for his job with the railroad. You met Sam. Then there's Boone."

Mama let out a long sigh.

"Boone apprentices with a surveyor. I think it is finally the right thing to keep his interest, and it lets him explore the territory."

"The other two boys?"

"Deacon is eighteen and Preston is almost seventeen. They are out with the herd today."

"You said you have a daughter?"

"Yes. Violet is eight. She's spending the day at the Glassman's. They have two girls, ages twelve and ten. Their mother is one of the Larson girls."

I tried to turn my attention back to the numbers in the account books. After trying to add up the same column four times, I closed the book.

I went outside to the clothesline. "Can I take your stuff to the cabin?"

Mama smiled and put a hand over her heart, like she did whenever I made her proud.

"Yes, that would be nice," she replied. "Should I go over and help clean it?"

"No. My cousins have it under control."

Truthfully, I just wanted a few minutes alone, away from everyone. I went inside and picked up her valise and satchel and strolled leisurely toward the cabin. Boone chased some-thing away with a stick. It was probably good that Ellie Mae did not witness that.

I poked my head in the small cabin. It had been years since I had been inside. When we saw Grandma Betty or Grandpa Ben, they came over to our house. I forgot how tiny the cabin seemed compared to our large home.

The cabin was only two rooms. The main room housed a small stove, a cupboard with a few dishes, a table with four chairs, and two wingback chairs with footstools. A small table with an oil lamp sat between the two chairs. I set the satchel on the dining table.

The other room had a bed, dresser, and nightstand. Penny and Dory already had the bedroom cleaned and fresh sheets and blankets on the bed, so I set Ellie Mae's valise in the bed-room.

"I think it is critter free now." Boone's loud voice echoed in the room.

Penny shooed us out so she could mop the floor. "We'll wash the curtains later this week. Hopefully Ellie Mae won't mind a little dirt until then."

"I think you've done a fine job making the place presentable," I said as I tweaked her nose.

As I walked around the far side of the lake, I wondered how long Ellie Mae Thatcher would stay. Then I wondered how much her presence would upset my routine. If I was to monitor her, then I figured wherever she went, I needed to follow her.

She waved to me as I rounded the lake, and I thought it might not be so bad to have my routine disrupted, especially if it meant seeing her pretty smile.

CHAPTER 5

ELLIE MAE

Supper at the Colter home was a noisy affair. Very different from my upbringing with only one brother. Violet stayed overnight at the Glassman's so I wouldn't meet her until the next day. However, I doubt if anyone noticed her absence. The three youngest Colter boys jostled for a seat next to me. Sam took the seat across from me and gave me an apologetic shrug.

I smiled. He was so quiet compared to his brothers, and I liked that about him. I also didn't mind looking at his amazing blue eyes all supper long.

Will said a blessing for the meal. As soon as it was over, I started the conversation, hoping to keep the topic off myself and on them.

"Hannah, Paul Lancaster told me you came west with the first governor's wagon train. What was that like?"

All the noise suddenly stopped.

"You did?" Preston asked, his light blue eyes widened. All four of her sons turned their attention to her.

She swallowed a bite of food and smiled at Preston. "I did. My first husband…"

Sam coughed and pounded his chest. Will reached over

and slapped his back.

"You okay, son?"

Sam nodded as his face turned bright red. "Sure."

"What do you mean, your first husband?" Boone frowned. It was the first time I'd seen his mood change away from jovial.

"Surely you boys know I met your papa here, in Arizona, right?"

I stuffed a bite of food in my mouth and chewed while I watched their reactions. Boone frowned. Sam looked at his plate and shifted in his chair. The two youngest stared with mouths open wide. It was kinda adorable.

Hannah seemed to gather her thoughts before she responded. "I grew up in Ohio and met Drew Anderson—"

"As in Thomas Anderson?" Boone thundered.

"Yes, Uncle Thomas is Drew's younger brother. I mean, he's not really your uncle. None of you are relatives to him. But he is Julia's girls' uncle by marriage. Your uncle by tradition."

I glanced over at Will. The hint of laughter crinkled his eyes, but he stifled it with some of his supper. Seemed like Hannah hadn't shared the story with the boys before.

"Anyway, Drew and I were married in Ohio. He was a doctor."

Sam cleared his throat. I could almost hear his thoughts. That tidbit gave him a fresh perspective of his mother.

"We came West on the same wagon train as the former Governor Goodwin. He wasn't the first governor."

Since I left my satchel by the door, I made a mental note about the governor. I figured they might think it rude if I took notes during the meal.

"We met the first governor, but not on the wagon train. His last name was Gurley. I have forgotten his first name.

He had an abscess that burst, and Drew treated him in his clinic. Unfortunately, all he could do was make the man comfort-able."

"Ewwww." Preston turned up his nose.

I listened carefully, hoping to commit the important de-tails to my memory.

I was going to ask Will a question so Hannah could eat, but Sam beat me to it.

"So, when exactly did you meet Mama?"

He looked pale and pushed his food around on his plate. Clearly, the conversation disturbed him.

Will smiled. "I met her here. It was '64, not long after she became widowed."

Will's eyes looked at Hannah. I could see the love in their gaze.

"I first met her when she was working at the mess hall at Fort Whipple. Though I didn't even say hi."

Hannah's smile faded, and she looked down at her plate. There was more to that story, but I would not push for de-tails. I was happy to hear anything they shared and content to let them keep what they wanted to themselves.

Will hesitated before he continued. "Anyway, the next time I met her was when she was working at Lancaster's boardinghouse."

Hannah smiled. "That was when I fished a bullet out of a man's leg."

Will slapped a hand on the table. "That's right. I forgot about that. You were beautiful and single, so I decided al-most immediately to win your heart."

"And you did," Hannah said as she took his hand in hers.

I smiled as my face warmed. I wanted that kind of love.

Will squeezed her hand. "We got married quickly after that. Then you boys came along."

Will winked at his wife, and her cheeks turned rosy. I sensed there were some pleasant memories going through her mind.

Throughout the meal, Sam kept shifting in his chair. He only ate a few bites of his food. Something bothered him. What I did not understand was why. Nothing his parents shared was disturbing.

When the meal finished, I offered to help with dishes, but Will said he wanted to help instead. He and Hannah whispered to each other. They lingered cleaning the dishes as they reminisced about the early days of their relationship.

Hoping not to intrude, I took my notebook and pencil and sat in the parlor. I wrote in my notes: the first governor wasn't the first. After more research, I would add details.

I was so engrossed in scratching down notes I did not no-tice Sam standing over me. He cleared his throat, and I looked up at him. I moved my leg so he could sit on the couch next to me, but he remained standing.

"Just how much of our personal lives are you going to publish?"

I sighed. He was not happy with me.

"My goal is to write engaging articles about the history of the early days of Prescott. I have no intention of airing any-one's skeletons from their closets, if that's what you mean."

"I don't think it is anyone's business that Mama was married before Papa. I can't see how mentioning it would be relevant."

I parsed my words carefully. The last thing I wanted to do was get into an argument with an overly protective son, no matter how handsome he was.

"It's really up to your mother. I will show her my articles before I send them to my editor. In fact, I'll show it to both your parents. If anything makes them uncomfortable, or if they think something is too personal, I'll be happy to re-work it."

"It won't do you any good to show Papa."

Finally, Sam sat down on the other end of the couch. He ran a hand through his hair.

"What do you mean?"

"He can't read. Or at least not anymore."

I frowned. I never heard of such a thing.

"This is not to end up in one of your stories, either." Sam glowered at me.

I set my pencil down to show him I was trustworthy.

"He hit his head before James was born. It left some permanent damage. The short version of the story is that he can't read."

I frowned. "But he returned my correspondence."

"As the manager of the ranch, I was the one who wrote that letter. Like I often do, I read it to him and then I signed his name when he blessed it."

I sat up straighter. "You mean to tell me you wrote that let-ter?"

He nodded. "That's part of the reason I was upset you were not a man. I reread your letter to make sure I wasn't responsible for the mistake. Papa was disappointed in me."

I shook my head. "He didn't seem like it earlier."

"You don't know him."

When Hannah and Will entered the parlor, Sam stood and let his mother sit on the couch with Will. I moved to a chair, so I could see them better. Will slid an arm around Hannah's shoulders. They must have been married for twenty-three years. I certainly hoped my husband would love me that much twenty years later.

"So," I said, recapping, "Hannah came west with her first

husband, who died on the journey."

Hannah nodded.

"How did you end up here, Will?"

He smiled and told us the story of how he left his father's ranch in Texas after his father died. He gave the broad version of the story but promised to tell about his other adventures from the trip later.

I scribbled notes, trying to keep up. When I yawned, I looked at the clock. It was nine o'clock.

"I'm so sorry for keeping you for so long. I should head to the cabin now."

Sam stood. So did his brothers.

"Sam will walk you over," Will said. He gave a warning look to his other sons. They slumped back in their seats.

I quickly stashed my things in my satchel and stood.

"You should take your meals with us," Hannah said. "We serve breakfast at seven."

"Thank you," I replied.

I placed my hand on Sam's arm and he led me out of the house into the darkness of night. He waited a moment, which gave my eyes a chance to adjust to the lower light.

"I hope it wasn't a mistake to invite you here," he said.

His words sliced into my heart. I had done nothing untrustworthy. Well, except conceal my gender in a letter.

He sighed heavily.

"What is on your mind?" I asked.

He led me along the dirt path toward the small cabin.

"I'm not sure I want to tell you. I wouldn't want it to show up in the paper."

"Sam, I have no ill motives. I want the best for you and your family. I don't know what I did to make you distrust me so much."

"You lied."

I took a deep breath. "I'm sorry. Obviously, my lie hurt you more than it did your parents."

He snorted but said nothing else.

When we arrived at the cabin, he waited for a moment. I stumbled around in the dark as I couldn't remember where the table was.

"Here." He followed me into the dark.

I tripped and fell down.

He stepped over me and lit the lamp on the table. Then he held out his hand to help me up.

"I'm sorry." My face burned. I was terribly uncoordinated in the dark.

When I placed my hand in his, tingles traveled up my arm. I think something happened to him too, because as soon as I was steady on my feet, he dropped my hand like a hot branding iron.

"Do you want me to escort you in the morning?" he asked.

I shook my head.

"Tomorrow, set the lamp over there." He pointed to a small table by the door. "That way you can light it right away and not hurt yourself."

"Thank you," I said as he stepped back out into the night. "Good night, Sam."

"Good night, Ellie Mae."

I closed the door behind him and took a stuttered breath. Even though he confused me, he made me feel like a princess. I didn't know what to do with that.

CHAPTER 6

SAM

As I walked back from Ellie Mae's cabin, I shook my arms, as if that could stop me from thinking about her dark eyes. In the low light of her cabin, they looked like dark pools that tempted me to move closer. I wanted to, despite my fear.

Almost kissing Ellie Mae wasn't my only fear. It scared me to learn about my parents' past. I didn't want to face the dark secret about myself. I knew there was one lurking beneath the surface. Most of all, I fretted that Ellie Mae would betray our trust, my trust.

My fear didn't make a lick of sense.

I shook my head as I opened the door. The house was quiet. As I entered the parlor, Mama patted the spot on the couch next to her. My brothers and papa retired upstairs.

"Come sit with me."

I did.

"What's bothering you?"

Mama could read me like a book. She knew I wrestled with something. She had a way of drawing thoughts and feelings out of me I could barely identify. I didn't know if all mamas were so gifted, or if mine was special.

"I didn't know you were married before."

She snorted. "I doubt very much that is really bothering you. I was sure you knew that, though. Surely, Will and I have told you the story of how we met."

I shook my head. If they had, I did not remember it.

"It's not important. Why does that bother you?"

"I don't know. Did you love him?"

"Drew? Yes. Very much."

My heart squeezed tight. "But you love Papa, right?"

I kicked myself for the question. My silly question made me sound like a little boy and not a man.

"I love your papa very much."

"I don't understand. How could you love them both?"

She laughed. "The same way I love each of you children. I have plenty of love in my heart, Sam."

She patted my leg. "The love I shared with my first husband was different, because he was a different man. He had different strengths and different weaknesses from Will. Our relationship was unique. But I loved him with my entire heart while he was alive. When he died, I took some time to get over my loss. Some of my friends thought I should marry the first man that noticed me. I didn't want that. I wanted to find love again. And I did, with your father."

I frowned. I didn't know why it bothered me so much, but it did.

"The connection I have with your father was instantaneous. Passionate."

"Ew."

She laughed. "Okay, too much detail. We fell in love quickly and deeply and our love grows year by year."

I sighed and picked some lint off my pants.

"I don't know why it bothers me. I guess I'm afraid I have disappointed Papa yet again." My shoulders sagged.

"What do you mean?"

"I'm pretty sure I disappointed him by not vetting Miss Thatcher better."

"I don't think he thinks that at all. Even if he could read, he would have handled it the same."

I wasn't sure I believed her.

"I'm sorry you feel you disappointed your papa. It could not be further from the truth. He is very proud of you. Like how you managed the stock purchase last month. He's proud of how you step up to every new challenge he throws at you. You are doing a great job with the finances of the ranch. He trusts you completely and sees that you have always been the best choice to run the ranch, regardless of birth order."

I let the words sink in for a few minutes.

"Why is it so hard to believe?" I asked.

Mama looked away. She didn't want to tell me what she knew.

She stood and yawned. Then I yawned.

"Don't be so hard on yourself, Sam. You are a good man. You deserve some happiness in your life."

She pointed to her cheek like she did when we were little boys. I kissed it and she hugged me. "Can you close up the house for the night?"

I nodded and watched as she disappeared upstairs. Then I secured the door, mostly to keep critters out. I left several windows open so the cool breeze would fill the house. I retired to my room after turning down the lamps.

When I opened the bedroom door, Boone's snores greeted me. I was glad he already slept, as I did not want to hear him talk about Ellie Mae.

I changed out of my clothes into some lightweight pajama shorts before sliding under the sheet. Unlike my brothers, I couldn't sleep buck naked. I always needed the sheet resting lightly over my legs and waist. They'd made fun of me for it all my life.

A few things became evident as I reflected on the day. The first was that Mama learned all her medical skills from her doctor husband. A lot of things suddenly made sense when she said he was a doctor.

Another thing was that I liked Ellie Mae. Even if I was mad at her for lying in her letter by omitting a few important details, I still liked her. Her eyes glowed when she smiled. When it was for me, my heart danced in my chest, like when I helped her up from the floor. Poor thing. I never saw a woman fall on the floor.

The last thing I learned: Mama knew a secret that might explain why I was the misfit in the family.

My mind gnawed on the secret Mama knew about me. I was torn. I wanted to know, but I was afraid of learning the truth. Did something happen in my past that I did not remember? Did it explain why I was afraid when it made no sense or why I felt apprehensive for no reason, like coming toward the ranch from the back way?

As long as I could remember, there were a handful of things like that. My heart would race if I was completely alone outside near the clothesline. I never could go stand there without someone else around. Riding a horse with someone else gave me the willies. I avoided risk, whereas most of my brothers ran headlong to embrace risk, though each to their own degree.

I rolled onto my side. Maybe someday I would feel like I really belonged in my family on the ranch.

CHAPTER 7

ELLIE MAE

The next day, I woke before dawn. If I had my typewriter, I would have written the first article. Unfortunately, it was still in Paul Lancaster's barn.

Before I could write the first article, I needed my typewriter and to research Mr. Gurley's background, both require-ed a trip into town. Also, the horse and saddle were due back to the livery.

I donned my light green calico dress. It hugged my meager, almost non-existent curves. God did not bless me with much of a bustline. At least the dress made my waist look small and my hips look curvy. I felt sorta feminine in it.

After brushing out my hair until it shone in the light, I twisted it into a knot at the base of my neck. I picked up my satchel and opened the front door.

"Morning."

I jumped at the sound of Sam's voice and placed a hand over my heart as my breathing returned to normal.

He pushed away from where he leaned against my cabin.

"I thought you were *not* escorting me to breakfast."

He shrugged. "That's a pretty dress."

My cheeks warmed as I placed my hand on the crook of his arm.

"If you're busy, you don't have to walk me to the house in the morning." Although, I had to admit, I liked it.

"No trouble."

He opened his pocket watch and glanced at the time before he stowed it in his vest pocket. He wore a gray vest and trousers with a white shirt. Just like the day before, his dark hair was slicked to one side, though part of it kept inching toward his eyes.

"Years ago," he said, "Mama would ring the dinner bell about now. When we hired a full-time cook for the bunkhouse, she stopped the practice."

"Oh?"

"She, Rosa, Aunt Mary, and Grandma Betty used to cook for most of the ranch. Maggie Larson handled her brood. I think after Grandma Betty passed and Aunt Mary got too busy running the school on the ranch, Mama focused on feeding us, especially since my brothers eat like we might run out of food any minute."

He laughed. It was a pleasant laugh that lit up his eyes.

"I should apologize in advance for the barbaric frenzy you are about to see."

I laughed. "I'll be careful to not get in the way."

"Not if you want to keep your limbs."

"I was wondering," I started. "Would you or one of your brothers take me into town? I need to return the horse and saddle to the livery, pick up my Remington, and check in with my editor."

"You shoot?"

"Oh, my Remington is not a gun. It's a typewriter."

"How big is it?"

"It will take up half the space on the table. It's heavier

than it is big."

"Yes, I can take you. I ought to pick up Violet and check in with the meat company, anyway. We can take the wagon."

I smiled. "Thank you."

I heard the noise long before we arrived at the porch. "I see what you mean about your brothers."

"Let me take your satchel for you," he said before he opened the door. "I'll set it in the parlor by my desk."

I nodded and braced myself for the aforementioned chaos. The noise was so loud I wanted to cover my ears. I glanced at Sam. His mouth turned downward, and he stepped around me to place my things in the parlor.

My jaw slackened as I watched the scene unfold. Boone had Preston in a headlock while Deacon tickled Preston's side. Preston squirmed and flailed his arms, trying to get his older brothers to stop. Boone rubbed his knuckles on the top of Preston's head, mussing his hair.

"Stop it!" Preston yelled between giggles.

"Boone!" Hannah's voice held a hard edge, which Boone ignored.

I thought if I announced my presence, they might settle down, so I said, "Morning, boys!"

It worked.

Deacon dropped his hands as Boone released Preston, who fell to the floor with a loud thud. He jumped to his feet and smoothed out his wrinkled shirt.

Boone stepped forward and ran a hand through his hair. "Morning, Ellie Mae."

Then he crossed over to the table and held a chair out for me. Sam held out a different chair, and I suddenly felt awkward. Will suggested that I sit at the foot of the table. Sam was the closest, so he held out that chair for me.

I smiled at him and took the offered seat.

Sam sat in the chair to my right while the others fought over the chair to my left.

"Boys." Will spoke the word calmly with authority. Immediately, Boone and Deacon sat down.

Hannah sighed and brushed a few strands of hair back from her forehead before she placed breakfast on the table. When she sat down, Will took her hand and squeezed it. He kept his hold as he bowed his head.

When the blessing ended, the noise returned. Boone reached over Deacon to snag the plate of bacon. He took an enormous pile and offered the plate to me. I took a few pieces and passed it over to Sam.

Deacon whined, "No fair."

Once everyone was served, Sam's brothers attacked their food. Sam, however, ate like a normal person. I held back a smile as I ate my breakfast.

"Papa," Sam started. "I'm going to take Ellie Mae into town today. She needs to return the rented horse and pick up her typewriter and check in with her editor. I'll need the wagon. I can pick up Violet, too."

Hannah smiled. "Oh, that's so kind of you."

Boone mocked his mother's response until he saw his father's deep scowl. I hid my smile behind my hand. Clearly, Boone was a rascal.

"You can take it," Will said.

"Typewriter?" Deacon asked, perking up.

Sam whispered to me, "He likes mechanical inventions. Just don't leave him alone with it 'cause he'll tear it apart and try to put it back together again."

"What kind is it?" Deacon asked.

"Remington 2, the 1878 edition," I answered.

"That must have set you back a pretty penny," Deacon

said. His knowledge surprised me.

"I'm not sure. It was a gift from my papa."

"So, it's the blind typewriter style, right, and not one of the ball styles?"

"Yes. I can show you later if you'd like."

He grinned. "Can I, Papa?"

Will nodded. "Just make sure Sam is with you."

Deacon's enthusiasm waned at the mention of his brother's name. He focused on his breakfast.

The conversation quieted as the boys inhaled their food. I wanted to get into town, so I focused on my meal.

When breakfast was complete, I offered to help with the dishes while Sam got the wagon ready. That time, Hannah accepted my offer.

Boone hovered while Sam and the two youngest headed out to the barn.

"If you think you'll need extra help, I can ride along with you," Boone said.

I held back a sigh. He might have been interested in me. I was not the least bit intrigued by him. He was the sort of boy my mama warned me away from.

"Doesn't Mr. Fremont need your help today?" Hannah asked.

Boone shrugged. "I'm sure it's fine if I miss a day."

Hannah set the dirty dishes in the sink and turned to face her stubborn son. "You will not shirk your responsibility. Mike Fremont is a good employer, and he is investing a lot of time to teach you his trade. You will not disrespect him."

Boone straightened his back and frowned. He stared his mother down. She took a step closer before he turned on his heel and stomped out the door.

Hannah let out a long sigh. "He's always pushing boundaries. Some days I just don't know what to do with

41

him. I pray the younger boys will transition to manhood easier than Boone is."

"It seems like Sam is the complete opposite of Boone," I said as I dried the dishes.

"Sam has been the easiest by far. He never challenged my authority or bucked responsibility. He is the most dependable of my boys."

She frowned but said nothing more. Something bothered her about Sam, but I would not press. She would tell me if she wanted to.

As I finished drying the last dish, Sam entered and announced the wagon was ready. I followed him outside.

How thoughtful. He pulled the wagon in front of the house. I could see why Hannah favored him. When he helped me up into the wagon, my face heated, and tingles ran up and down my arm. Every time he was close to me, my senses heightened. I was very aware of him.

He joined me on the other side. When he set the wagon in motion, I caught a whiff of cedar from him. The smell fit him. Practical. Simple.

As we rode into town, neither of us said much. I enjoyed the beautiful drive sitting next to him. Even though he did not invite me to place my hand on the crook of his arm, I really wanted to.

I glanced at him. His gaze remained steadfastly facing forward. I wondered if he was ever around any women, much less one not related to him. He seemed stiff and uncomfortable until the outskirts of the town became visible.

"Where would you like me to drop you off?" he asked.

"At the newspaper office. Can I meet you over at Lancaster's in an hour?" I asked.

He looked at his pocket watch. "Let's say eleven o'clock?"

I nodded as he pulled the wagon to a stop in front of the Prescott Gazette office. I did not wait for him to help me down since I was capable.

"I would have helped you." He sounded disappointed.

"I know. I didn't want to delay your errands."

"You said the horse and saddle were Thomas Anderson's, right?"

I nodded.

"I'll drop them off for you."

"Thank you."

Our eyes locked. Neither one of us was eager to move on with our errands. At length, he moved the wagon forward again. I sighed as he pulled away.

Then I turned and entered the building. I found my editor, Clayton Williams, in his office.

"Morning," I said.

He looked up and smiled. "You have something for me already?"

I dug around in my satchel and handed him the introduction piece I typed up before leaving my home in Chino Valley. "I know you already ran two of my articles, but I thought this might set the stage for the full series."

His eyes scanned the article. He marked a few notes on the page. Then he smiled and handed the paper back to me. "Just a few minor changes and we can run it."

I scanned his notes. I misspelled two words. That was it. I handed the paper back to him.

"I like how you tied hope for a new life to the reason people move here. That's fantastic for the paper and the town."

"Thank you. Can you tell me where to find information about the first governor, Mr. Gurley? He never made it here, so the President appointed Goodwin instead."

"There is a section on territorial history in our library," Clayton said. "I'd start there."

The small library was in the room next to Clayton's office. After I told the clerk what I was looking for, he helped me find it. I took the archived documents over to a table and studied them before I added the relevant facts to my note-book.

After I finished my research, I promised to return in a few days with the next article. Then I walked over to the Lancaster's boardinghouse.

Paul and Millie greeted me and asked how I was doing. We visited for a bit on the front porch until Sam joined us.

I watched as he stepped down from the wagon and walked toward us. His stride was confident. A bowler hat shaded his eyes. It amazed me that a man who grew up on a ranch could look like a city fella. Yet, it seemed to fit his personality.

When he arrived at the bottom of the porch stairs, a smile spread across his face. I could not help but smile back as my heart warmed. I really liked his smile.

"Have you eaten?" he asked.

I shook my head.

"Can I take you over to Isabel's Café for lunch?"

"Don't you need to pick up your sister?"

He smiled. "We can pick her up after lunch. Knowing her, she will want to eat with her friends."

He held out his hand. I said my farewells to the Lancasters and put my hand in his. Warmth spread through me until he released his hold and tucked my hand in the crook of his arm.

I think I was falling for Sam Colter.

CHAPTER 8

SAM

When I left Eddie and Annabel at the butcher's shop, Annabel suggested I should take Ellie Mae to lunch. She saw us ride into town together.

I thought about the idea and when I spotted Ellie Mae sitting on the porch with the Lancasters; I decided it would be nice to have her to myself for a quiet meal. Violet would be fine for a few more hours with her friends.

When she took my offered hand, my breath caught in my throat. Every time I touched her, my pulse quickened, and currents ran through my limbs. I released a quiet breath when she put her hand in the crook of my arm.

"Did you grow up around here?" I asked, trying to distract myself from the effect of her nearness.

"My father is a farmer in Chino Valley. We moved there when I was a little girl, and my younger brother was a baby."

That explained the postmark on her letter.

We were seated by the windows at the front of the restaurant. Ellie Mae removed her hat and placed it on the chair next to her. I did the same. The sunlight from the window cast a golden glow on her hair. Her eyes sparkled as she looked at me.

"What do you recommend?" she asked as she set the menu aside.

I laughed. "I'm the business manager for a ranch and butcher, so I will always recommend anything with beef in it."

Her face lit up with a full smile, exposing her beautiful straight teeth. "Then I will order a roast beef sandwich."

"Excellent choice."

The server took our order and left.

Words left me as I suddenly felt very self-conscious under Ellie Mae's scrutiny.

"So, you are the businessman," she said. "Boone is a surveyor."

"And troublemaker."

She giggled. "Yes, I noticed that. Deacon likes to take things apart. What is Preston's talent?"

Being teased by Boone. I figured it was best not to voice that opinion. "I think he's still figuring it out."

"And your older brother, James, he's a railroad man?"

"Yes. He has followed all the news about the railroads since he could first read. The moment he was old enough to leave home, he moved to southern Arizona for a job with the Southern Pacific Railway. Now he is the Superintendent of Transportation for the Central Arizona Railway."

Our food arrived, so I said a blessing over it. Then I picked up my sandwich and started eating.

"What do you like to do in your free time?" she asked.

As I chewed my food slowly, I considered her question. I never considered what I liked to do. I just did what my parents expected of me.

She took a bite of her roast beef sandwich. "Mmm. This is good."

"I guess I like to read." I read a lot in the evenings.

"What types of things?"

"I usually read the newspaper and magazines about ranching or the railroad. Sometimes a dime novel."

Her eyes lit up. "What genre?"

I never thought about it. "I will read just about anything. If I don't like the story, then I stop reading it."

She laughed. "I guess that makes sense."

"What do you like to do?" I asked.

"I devour anything I can get my hands on about history, especially our country's history. I like western dime novels with a bit of a love story."

"So, no crocheting or knitting?" I teased her.

She laughed. "Knitting is like a chore to me. I can, if needed, but I'd much rather read."

I smiled. Ellie Mae was easy to talk to. She told me more about the farm where she grew up and her parents and brother. When I finally paid for our meal, it was after one.

"We should go," I said reluctantly. I could have spent the whole day with her.

We headed back over to the boardinghouse. Paul loaded Ellie Mae's typewriter and her trunk into the wagon. Then I drove us over to the Glassman's house to pick up Violet.

When I knocked on the door, their nanny greeted me. Then she fetched Violet.

"Come on, squirt," I greeted my little sister.

"Who's that?" Violet asked when she saw Ellie Mae.

"Her name is Ellie Mae. She's a journalist and our guest."

I lifted Violet into the back of the wagon.

"Hello, Violet," Ellie Mae greeted her. "How was the visit with your friends?"

Violet immediately opened up. She recounted her visit with great detail. I dropped Violet's things in the back of the wagon and pointed the horses toward home. I was glad I took Ellie Mae to lunch, because my sister monopolized the conversation the entire way home.

When we arrived back at the ranch, Papa came out to greet Violet. He led her into the ranch house, which freed me up to drive the wagon over to the cabin.

I helped Ellie Mae down from the wagon, which triggered fluttery feelings in me again. She held the door for me as I carried her trunk to her bedroom. I did not linger there. I put the typewriter in the main part of the house. It was heavier than I thought it would be.

"I'll be back soon with something to open the crate," I said.

I drove the horses and wagon back over to the barn. I cared for them before I found a crowbar and returned to the cabin.

Her voice sounded far away when I knocked. She was unpacking her trunk in her bedroom. I pried the top off the crate. Then I moved the straw away to reveal the typewriter.

She stood next to me and sighed dreamily. "I missed it. I know it sounds silly. Once I got used to writing with it, I found it's hard to go back to pen and paper."

"You want me to find another table for it?"

"No. You can put it on the dining table. I doubt I'll be entertaining anyone while I'm here."

I swallowed and begged my heart to slow down. Then I lifted the heavy thing out of the crate and set it down.

"Perfect. Thank you."

A part of me wanted to linger there with her. I thought about what it would be like if I kissed her. Then I remembered Papa asked me to watch out for her, so something like that did not happen.

I excused myself and took the empty crate to the barn. Then I picked up the mail and other things I had set on my papa's workbench when I put the wagon away earlier.

When I returned, Mama greeted me before I went into the parlor to work. As I glanced at the clock, I realized I wouldn't get much work done as late as it was, so I flipped through the mail.

"Sam!" Deacon called as he entered the room.

I sighed. I just finished looking through the mail.

"Is it here? The typewriter?"

"Yes. It's in Ellie Mae's cabin."

"Come on. I want to see it."

I remembered Papa told him I had to go with, so I stood and walked with him back to Ellie Mae's cabin. The sound of keys striking paper greeted us when I opened the door. Dea-con lunged forward, but I grabbed his arm.

"Wait. Let her finish what she's working on."

"Just a minute," she greeted us. A minute later, she said, "I'm finished. You can come over now."

I nodded, and Deacon rushed over to see the contraption. He walked around the machine and studied it.

"It's an understrike, so how do you see what you typed?" he asked. I found myself just as curious.

"You lift the carriage here." She showed him.

His eyes cataloged every nuance of the machine. I watched him do the same with other machinery, like Mama's wash ringer. Deacon looked under the carriage and touched the metal cables strung to the keys.

"It has a shift key," Ellie Mae said. "So, I can type full sentences with the initial capital letters."

"Oh!" Deacon exclaimed. "Can I try it?"

Ellie Mae stood and leaned over his shoulder to show him how to load the paper. I was a little jealous of how close she was to my brother.

Deacon loaded the paper. "My name is Deacon," he said as he found the letters. "I read about this QWERTY letter arrangement. It's supposed to help you type faster."

He pulled the paper from the machine and examined the type. Then he folded the paper and put it in his pocket. He was so careful; I wondered if he might frame it.

"Do you type fast?" he asked as he stood.

"Yes. With practice, you could too. Do you want to try?" Ellie Mae asked me.

I was not one to try new things, but I sat down and let her lean over me like she did to Deacon. My heart thrummed within my chest when her hand brushed mine as she reached for a sheet of paper. She cleared her throat, and I wondered if she felt what I did.

"What should I type?" I asked.

"Anything you want," she said.

I smiled and found the keys to type: I enjoyed our lunch. I would like to go again soon.

When I finished, she reached over and pulled out the paper. When she read it, pink colored the apples of her cheeks.

"That's for you," I said.

She smiled and folded the paper.

"What does it say?" Deacon asked.

I stood. "That's for Ellie Mae to know."

Deacon fussed for a few seconds, then turned his attention back to the machine. He mumbled to himself. "A better design would let you see as you type."

Neither Ellie Mae nor I would have noticed if he said that the cabin was burning down. Her eyes locked with mine. My gaze roamed over her hair, her eyes, her lips.

"What's wrong with you?" Deacon asked as he destroyed the moment.

A noise came from the doorway. "It's suppertime," Boone announced.

I tore my gaze away from Ellie Mae and offered her my arm. As she put her hand in the crook of my arm, I covered it with mine.

"Thank you," she whispered.

I was not sure if she thanked me for the note or bringing her typewriter. Either way, my heart soared as we walked over to the ranch house.

CHAPTER 9

ELLIE MAE

One never imagines when she embarks on a new adventure in life that it might lead to the unexpected joy of falling in love. I wasn't thinking about it when I came to the ranch. I was there to start my career as a journalist.

Yet, the moment that Sam handed me his first typewritten note, I thought I might be falling in love with him. Of all the things he could have chosen for his first typewritten words, he chose words for me.

I still have the note tucked away in a special box.

It annoyed me we were not alone. I would have liked him to kiss me then. Instead, I took his arm and followed his younger brothers over to the ranch house with Sam by my side.

We entered the house, and he took me straight to the foot of the table. He sat on my right and Violet sat on my left. I was glad not to have his brothers jockeying for that position.

Nothing noteworthy happened during the meal. The Colters talked about their day. After the meal finished, I help-ed Hannah with the dishes. Then we sat in the parlor.

"Tell me about the early days," I said.

"When me and the cowboys first arrived," Will said, "it was tough. We were shorthanded. Building the bunkhouse and the log cabin was hard work. At night, campfire lit the hills and out toward the horizon. Had a scuffle with Indians at one point. But we survived."

"What about when you were first married?" I asked.

Hannah sighed. "The first year seemed like a blur. Rosa and I worked very hard to keep up with the cooking and cleaning. I was used to it, having worked at Lancaster's Boardinghouse."

She smiled at Sam. "Once James and Samuel were born, life got more difficult. They were two weeks shy of being a full year apart."

"I remember when they got chicken pox. Neither of them slept through the night."

"I remember that," Will said. "I don't think either of us slept much after Sam was born for the first six months."

"Once he was old enough to sleep through the night," Hannah said, "he got chicken pox and a fever, so we were back to sleepless nights."

"By the time the boys improved…" Hannah stopped.

"There was the kidnapping." Will said it so calmly. Despite his tone, a shadow came over his face and Hannah's.

"Kidnapping?" Preston asked as he leaned forward.

I looked over at Sam. He straightened in his chair. His jaw twitched, and he flattened his palms against his knees.

"What happened?" Boone asked.

Will glanced at Hannah. She nodded.

"My brother hired some men to kidnap Hannah, James, and Sam. Only the kidnappers ended up with Hannah, Sam, and your cousin Eddie, my brother's son."

Sam cleared his throat. "What route… How did they leave the ranch?"

I observed Sam as Hannah answered. "I hung laundry on the clothesline. Sam was in a bassinet. Eddie was around somewhere. They came upon me and told me to grab Sam. They already had Eddie."

She cleared her throat and turned compassionate eyes toward Sam. "We skirted the lake and went up over the hill. The back way out of the ranch."

Sam's hands fisted, and his face went pale. Will clasped Hannah's hand.

"We were on horseback. I convinced the men to take a break because it was hard to carry Sam. I fashioned a sling to hold him close. He was only four or five months old."

Sam stared at the corner of the room.

"That explains why he's your favorite," Boone said.

"Boone," Will warned his son with a growl.

Hannah frowned.

Will took over the storytelling. "My brother purchased a ranch out past Wickenburg. His men took them there. Me, Warren, and several of the cowboys met up with Perry Quinn and his men. It was back in the day when Perry owned a ranch in the valley. We finally picked up the trail after several days."

Hannah added, "Reuben held me, Sam, and Eddie in a shack on his property. Finally, Will found us."

"There was a shootout," Will said.

"Warren killed Reuben to save me. To save us," Hannah said.

The room was silent. I never heard such silence from the Colter boys. I looked around the room. Sam looked like he was ready to bolt. Boone crossed his arms and frowned. Deacon and Preston sat wide-eyed as if they could not believe what they just heard. Violet moved to sit next to Hannah and leaned into her side. Will put his arm around Hannah and held her tight. They watched Sam.

I followed their gaze. His face made subtle changes. First shock. Then confusion. Then anger.

He stood abruptly. The sound of his boots clomping along the wood floor seemed loud in the silence. He raced out of the house.

Hannah stood, but Will gripped her arm.

"Let him go."

The brothers shifted.

"Things make more sense now," Boone said. He turned his gaze toward Hannah. "Like why he can do no wrong in your eyes."

Will stood and blocked Boone's view of Hannah. Boone pressed his lips into a firm line. Then he left the house. A few minutes later, we heard the thundering of his horse's hooves.

"Would you care for some lemonade?" Hannah asked me.

"That would be nice," I said even though I didn't want any. She obviously needed to do something.

Will followed her into the kitchen.

I was relieved when Deacon and Preston started whispering and jostling each other. Whatever they said did not matter as much as they returned to normal.

Shifting in my seat, I felt incredibly uncomfortable. I never expected such a story. Not in a million years. It would be a great idea for my novel, but I would not use it in an article, especially since it upset Sam. Boone, well, I wasn't really worried about his feelings. He seemed the type to bounce back quickly.

"I should talk to him." Hannah's voice came from the kitchen.

"He needs time to sort this out." Will's soft words filtered into the parlor.

I was not sure what to do. I felt like I was eavesdropping. Since no lemonade was being made, I picked up my things. There wouldn't be more stories that night.

I made a lot of noise as I walked past the dining room. "Thank you for supper," I said. It seemed lame to say it. "I'm going to call it a night."

I did not wait for a response. Instead, I opened the door and stepped onto the porch. I waited a moment for my eyes to adjust to the darkness.

Though I wished Sam would escort me home, especially since I was terrible at finding my way in the dark, there was no chance I was going to look for him or disturb him. I was confident he was very unhappy with me.

CHAPTER 10

SAM

Kidnapped. Someone had kidnapped me.

The moment I heard the word, many things about my life made sense.

I stood and ran out the door unsure where to hide. There was the barn, but the hay made me sneeze and my eyes water. If I sat on the porch, someone would find me. I considered walking around the lake, but it reminded me of the route my kidnappers took.

So, I walked towards Ellie Mae's cabin. I hid behind the large rock just beyond it so no one would find me if they came looking. 'Course a rattlesnake might, but that did not matter right then. As I sat down, I leaned my head back against it and looked up at the stars in the sky.

I cursed.

I never cursed. I was the obedient son. The dependable one. The risk-adverse one.

I snorted.

Risk-adverse. That made sense. Before my first birthday, I experienced more risk than most faced in a decade.

I rubbed my hand over my face.

Then rage coursed through me. My mother lied to me.

She knew something was wrong with me and that I did not belong in my family. She knew the reason, but never breathed a word.

Instead, she made up for it by giving me special attention. She coddled me. Favoritism was actually her compensating for what happened to me as a babe. Maybe it had been to assuage her guilt for the kidnapping. I did not know.

I picked at a long piece of grass on the ground next to me and plucked it in half. Then I threw it and grabbed another.

For the first time in my life, I wished for a nice long brawl with Boone, even though he would best me.

The anxiety that I lived with for my entire life made complete sense. Of course, I had been afraid when they kidnapped me. I was only a baby and had no way of identifying that. No wonder I hated the laundry area near the clothesline. No wonder the hair on the back of my neck stood on end when I took the trail up the mountain on the far side of the lake.

Everything made sense.

A noise came from behind me. I strained to listen.

"Ow." Ellie Mae's voice drifted up the path. "Oh!"

I rolled my eyes. The woman was clumsier than an ox in the dark. I should go help her. But I did not.

If E. M. Thatcher never came to our home, I would not be stewing over the biggest shock of my life. No, I would be in blissful ignorance. Ignorance was where I longed to return to.

I heard her sigh heavily. Then fall.

Shoot. Papa would have my hide if he found out I was out there and did not help her.

I stood and coughed to announce my presence.

"Who's there?" Her voice held a tinge of fear.

"It's me."

I found her a few feet away on the ground. I felt for her arms in the darkness, and I hauled her to her feet. Of course, fire raced up my arms from the touch. Blast it all.

"You alright?" I did not really want to know.

"I... Yes."

I walked her to her door.

"Thank you," she whispered.

I grunted.

She opened the door and lit a lamp. Then she stood in the doorway and looked at me. Her look of compassion stirred my anger.

"I'm sorry," she said.

"You should be. If it weren't for you..." I growled. I couldn't even find the words to argue properly. I turned to walk away.

She grabbed my arm and stepped out of her cabin.

"Sam."

I shook off her hand. Then I turned to face her. I couldn't brawl with her like I would with my brothers, but I could joust with words.

"I wish you never came here. You and your lies."

Shock turned to hurt. I did not care. I needed to vent some-where, and she was there.

"You are a horrible person, E. M. Thatcher. You waltzed into my perfectly fine life and, with just a few innocent questions, turned it entirely upside down."

"Sam." She tried to reach for me again, but I stepped back. I saw the sorrow in her face. I ignored it.

"Why? Why did you come here? So, you could get some dirt on my family? On me? And then air it to the whole town?"

A tear trickled down her cheek, glistening in the light from her doorway. I should stop. I was hurting the woman I was falling in love with.

Instead, I plowed forward in rage.

"I hate you, Ellie Mae! You disgust me."

Then I turned and stormed back toward the house. I stopped before going inside. I could not chance hiding in my room. Boone could be there. So, I sat on one of the rocking chairs on the porch.

Feeling a little remorse for my harsh words to Ellie Mae, I ran a hand through my hair.

If she never visited the ranch, the kidnapping would still be a secret. I would not be angry, hurt, or confused. I would not understand what was wrong with me. Once I knew, I wished I did not.

Until my rage simmered to a smoldering ember, I sat there for some time. The sounds of the house grew quiet. Lights dimmed.

As I looked towards Ellie Mae's cabin, I saw her light was still on. I wondered if she typed up a revealing article that would hurt me or my family.

I resolved to interact with her as little as possible. Hopefully, she would leave our home soon so I could get back to my normal life.

CHAPTER II

ELLIE MAE

When Sam walked away from my door, I laid down on my bed and cried. I thought he liked me. He gave me that note. That sweet note that softened my heart toward him.

Instead, he hated me. He blamed me.

I rolled over onto my side. He might never forgive me. Even if I was not at fault, the only way to move past it would be if he forgave me.

The hole it tore through my heart hurt. I needed to write.

I went out to the table and sat down in front of my typewriter. I loaded a piece of paper, and I wrote.

Words came forth in rapid sentences. The heroine of my novel was heartbroken. She felt the utter pain and rejection that I felt. It poured forth. Page after page after page.

He was angry with her. She longed for things to be different.

My heart bled through their story.

Finally, the words slowed. My energy faded. My eyes drooped.

I pulled the last sheet from the typewriter and set it on the stack of heartfelt words that bared my soul. Then I turned down the lamp, changed into my nightgown, and went to bed.

The next morning, I woke later than normal. I was not sure how late I stayed up typing. I walked to my bedroom win-dow, which faced the ranch house. Will, Deacon, and Preston walked toward the barn. A few minutes later, the three of them rode out toward the herd. I missed breakfast.

I washed up and dressed for the day in my brown skirt and white blouse. Then I loosely coiled my hair on top of my head. I scrounged around the cupboards and found some coffee grounds and a coffee pot. I went outside to the water pump and filled the coffeepot. Then I lit a fire in the stove and set the coffeepot on it.

As I waited for my coffee to brew, I flipped through the pages I typed last night. Thirty pages. That was the most I had written in one sitting. I scanned some scenes. It was good. The story deviated some from my original plan for the plot, but it was better than what I initially intended.

My coffee was ready, so I poured a cup and sat down in front of my typewriter. I needed to write my article. I re-trieved my notes about the first territorial governor, the one that never made it. Then I wrote the article.

Sam's words rolled around in my mind. He hated me.

So, I omitted naming his mother as the source of the ar-ticle. I merely said that a doctor and his wife were on the wagon train with Governor Goodwin. People who knew the story firsthand knew it was Hannah. Otherwise, no one would guess it was her.

I ended the article with a flourish about the sad reality of the wagon train. I reread the article, tweaked some of my word usage, then typed up a fresh copy.

A knock sounded at my door. I stood and answered it.

"Morning," Hannah greeted me. "I thought you could

use some breakfast."

She held out a plate of cold food.

"Come in."

I took the plate and set it next to my typewriter.

"It's been years since I've been out here. How do you like it?"

I held up the coffeepot, and she nodded. I poured her a cup and placed it on a corner of the table.

"Sorry, this takes up a lot of space." I moved my manuscript to the seat of one of the unused chairs. Then I offered her a seat.

"Looks like you've written a lot."

I swallowed a bite of the cold eggs. "Thanks, by the way. I stayed up working on my novel last night."

"A novel?"

"I doubt I will ever get published, but it is my dream. The story came to me last night, so I felt compelled to type it up."

Hannah sipped the coffee as I ate some of the bacon.

"I was worried when you missed breakfast. I hoped you were not upset with me or Will."

I snorted. "I am not the one who is upset with anyone."

My eyes drifted to the window. "Sam hates me."

"What makes you say that?"

My gaze connected with hers. "He found me stumbling home and told me as much."

Her eyes went wide. Then her lips turned down. "I'm so sorry."

"You're not to blame."

"Oh, but I think I am. I'm certain he is angry with me, and he took it out on you."

I swallowed more food. "Why would he be angry with you?"

She turned the mug around in her hands. When the handle pointed at her right hand again, she took another sip. Then she lowered the cup to the table.

"Sam believes there is something wrong with him because he is nothing like his brothers. He's asked me about it many times. I suspected the kidnapping shaped how he views life. But I didn't see how knowing about that would help him. I may have been wrong. It may have helped him understand why he is the way he is."

I finished eating. Then I took her hand and squeezed it. "You could not have known. That's a difficult situation. No matter how or when it came out, it was going to hurt."

"I hoped he would never know. As soon as we started telling the story, I realized my mistake."

I smiled at Hannah. She was such a kind soul. She loved her sons deeply. That was obvious from the start.

She sighed. "I'm sorry he took it out on you. I think he likes you."

Heat warmed my face. I thought about his note on my nightstand. I thought he liked me too.

Hannah laughed. "I see you might like him too."

I nodded. I could not pretend otherwise.

"Give him some time. If there is one thing I know about Sam, he will eventually tire of chewing over things in his mind. He will realize his mistake and make things right. It might just take some time."

"I have my first article, if you'd like to review it?" I handed her the clean version I finished right before she arrived.

"Oh, I trust you."

"You and Will should read it. I'll have time to fix it this evening if it is too personal."

She took the paper. Then she stood and took my empty

plate and silverware. "Will we see you for lunch?"

"Yes. I will join you for lunch after I finish some writing. And thanks again for breakfast."

After Hannah left, I typed up a second article based on Will's stories about his trip to Arizona and what he and his men endured while constructing buildings and trying to manage the herd. I glanced at the clock on the wall, and it was almost noon.

I grabbed the second article and hurried down the path to the ranch house.

When I opened the door, Hannah, Will, and Violet sat at the table.

"I'm sorry I'm late. I was just finishing this," I said, handing the article to Hannah.

Will frowned. I probably should have handed it to him, but it seemed cruel to do so, knowing he could not read.

"Sam told me about…"

Will nodded. "Have a seat."

I sat and felt a little uncomfortable until he blessed the meal.

"Where's Sam?" I asked.

Hannah smiled. "He said he had an errand in town."

Will grumbled. "I don't know why he didn't just take care of it yesterday."

"Ellie Mae," Violet said, "do you like wildflowers?"

I smiled and was glad for the distraction. "I do."

"Mama, can I pick some flowers for Ellie Mae this afternoon?"

"Yes, you may, Vi."

"I like flowers too," Violet said. "Papa, do you want some flowers?"

Will chuckled. "That's alright, Vi. You can pick some for your mama and Ellie Mae. We'll put them in a vase on the table at supper."

"That would be nice," Violet said.

When she said something else, Hannah asked her to eat her meal.

"It's laundry day," Hannah said as she looked at me. "Do you have anything that needs washed?"

"I do. I would be happy to help. Now that I finished my articles, I can take the afternoon off."

After we finished lunch, Will stayed for a while longer. When Hannah read my articles to him, I excused myself. I went back to the cabin to get my laundry. By the time I returned to the ranch house, Will left.

"What did he think?" I asked. My hands sweat and my face heated.

"He loves them. You are a talented writer, Ellie Mae."

"So, no changes?"

Hannah shook her head. "None. Thanks for leaving my name out of the one about the first governor. But I would not mind if you mentioned me by name."

"That's good to know. I think Sam would be upset if I included your name."

"That was very thoughtful of you."

Hannah retrieved her family's laundry, and we went outside to wash everything. Violet picked flowers nearby.

An idea formed in my head. Hannah said that Sam liked me, which meant he did not really mean the words he spewed at me last night. If I did something special for him, it would smooth things over.

"What is Sam's favorite dessert?" I asked.

"Pie of any kind. I think he especially likes cherry," Hannah said. Her eyes lit up. "I have some canned cherries in the pantry. Are you thinking we should make him cherry pie?"

"Would you mind if I borrowed your kitchen?" I asked.

"When we're done here, you can make Sam a cherry pie. I'll make a peach pie for the other boys."

I smiled. It was the perfect plan. I enjoyed having Hannah as an ally.

As we hung the clothes on the line to dry, a horse rode down the trail by the lake. Hannah called it the back way to the ranch.

"That's Sam and his pinto, Bailey."

I watched as he pulled his horse up in front of the barn. Then he led it inside. I wondered how he would handle me in the kitchen with his mama while he tried to work in the par-lor.

I shrugged off the thought and followed Hannah back in-side. Violet came with us. Her arms were full of enough wild-flowers for two vases.

As Hannah and I started working on the pies, Sam entered. Without a word, he went into the parlor and sat down at his desk. I really hoped cherry pie was his favorite, because some-thing needed to thaw his frosty glare.

CHAPTER 12

SAM

I still stewed the morning after the kidnapping revelation. Ellie Mae did not show up for breakfast. That was fine with me.

Until Mama looked at me. I hid nothing from her. She pierced me with her eyes. My cheeks flushed, and I looked away. I was pretty sure she knew I did something wrong. No way was I gonna talk about it at breakfast in front of my brothers and sister. Nor in front of Papa.

When breakfast was done, I lied and said I needed to go into town. I was pretty sure neither Papa nor Mama believed that was the truth, especially since I had just taken Ellie Mae to town the day before.

That day felt like five days ago. So much had happened.

I saddled Bailey and pointed him in the general direction of town with no apparent purpose but to escape for a few hours.

My mind took me to the butcher shop. Annabel greeted me with a warm smile.

"Sam, did you forget something yesterday?"

"No. Is Eddie around?"

"He's out back putting some meat in the smoker. You

COLTER SONS BOOK 1

can go on back."

I headed that way. I guess my mind sought out the other kidnapped child.

"Morning," I announced my presence to my cousin.

"Sam, this is a surprise. Something wrong?"

I kicked at some dirt on the ground. "I got something on my mind."

He smiled. "I'm surprised you came to me."

"It's got to do with something you and I both experience-ed."

Eddie frowned. He opened the door to the smokehouse and placed several large briskets in the shack. The smoke wafted out toward me. I moved to avoid getting a face full of it.

After a few minutes, he closed the smokehouse door.

"Care for some iced tea?" he asked as he washed his hands and arms. He removed his butcher's apron and motioned me toward his house behind the butcher shop.

He offered me a seat on the porch. Then he came out with two glasses of iced tea. It was a treat to have the ice in it. I sip-ped on the refreshing liquid.

"What's on your mind?" Eddie asked.

"Mama and Papa told us about the kidnapping."

Eddie frowned and set his glass down on the small table between us.

"Why would they do that?" His voice held an edge. It might have been a mistake to seek him out.

"There's a journalist staying with us. She's writing arti-cles about the early days of Prescott. She was asking ques-tions and somehow Papa blurted it out."

Eddie took a deep breath. "And what do you want from me?"

"Is it true?"

"If they told you my dead father kidnapped us, then yes. If they told you Warren killed him, then yes, it's true."

I looked over at him. A vein in his neck bulged. His hand tightened around the arm of the chair.

Obviously, it bothered him. I felt bad for mentioning it. I had not thought that through.

"I'm sorry for bringing it up." I stood and started to leave.

"Wait!" Eddie followed me and steered me back toward the porch chair. "It is a terrible memory for me. My father was a wicked man. He deserved what he got. But he was still my father. I struggled to get over it. So, it shocked me when you said something about it out of the blue."

He sat down and offered me a seat. "You came all this way. Might as well talk to me."

"How old were you?" I asked.

"I think I was eight years old."

I frowned. I pressed on, even though I didn't know what I hoped to gain.

"What do you remember about it?"

Then Eddie told me the story. He filled in some details that Mama failed to recount. James was supposed to be the other child kidnapped, not Eddie. His father had been angry about that. He also thought his father meant to hurt my mama. It was hard to reconcile what he thought he knew about his father with whom his father really was.

Eddie's story put mine into perspective. I was too young to remember when it happened. He dealt with the memories of living through it.

"You've known me all my life," I said. "Do you think I am the way I am because of the kidnapping?"

Eddie rubbed a hand over his beard. "You might be on to something. You have always been very cautious. That experience might have brought it out in you. But I also think you are you, because that's how God made you. The good parts of who you are—that's a gift. Your parents love you and appreciate your groundedness, unlike James and Boone. In their old age, you will be the one who cares for them. You will work alongside your father at the ranch like you are now. He trusts you more than the others."

Eddie laughed. "'Course you tell any of them I ever said so, I'll deny it. I don't play favorites with my cousins."

I laughed.

"Can I give you some advice as your older and wiser cousin?"

I nodded.

"Let loose. Live a little. Let the past roll off your shoulders and fall away from you. Carrying it around does no good. Just makes you and everyone around you miserable. If Annabel and I carried the past with us, we would not have a good life or marriage."

Eddie stood. I did too.

Then he slapped me on the shoulder. "The stuff churning inside of you is part of what it means to become a man. Decide what you will hold on to and let the rest go. That's thinking like a man instead of thinking like a boy."

I thanked him even though the words hurt. I knew he meant them for my good. That was Eddie. Always seeing and saying the good.

As I walked around front to collect Bailey, I thought about that. My cousin wrestled with the kidnapping more than I had any right to. He came to terms with his papa's evil nature and that his step-papa killed him.

I shook my head. My papa was a godly man. My mama loved me and prayed for me. Sure, I experienced something awful as a baby. But I could choose not to be a miserable person and let go of my pain.

I wasn't ready to. It meant I ought to apologize to Ellie Mae.

Unwilling to deal with that yet, I mounted Bailey and headed down the road by the stockyards which was the back way. At least I faced one thing head on.

When I noticed Ellie Mae and Mama at the clothesline, I skirted around the lake and headed straight for the barn. I brushed Bailey down, hoping to delay my next encounter with Ellie Mae. I sneezed several times as the smell of hay seemed stronger than normal.

At last, I headed toward the house, unable to postpone a greeting any longer. When I opened the door to the house, I caught sight of Mama and Ellie Mae in the kitchen. Mama placed her arms around Vi, showing her how to knead the dough. Looked like pie dough.

Ellie Mae smiled.

I schooled my face to be impassive. Anything else required an apology from me. Stubbornness still entrenched me.

I marched into the parlor and sat down at my desk. Vi's giggles and Mama's laughter were hard to ignore as I opened the books. I wanted to look over my shoulder to see if Ellie Mae looked as jovial as them.

Instead, I calculated figures in the ledger. I entered a slew of receipts from the butcher shop and summed them up. Then I stood and worked some kinks out of my back.

When I turned around, Ellie Mae was gone. Vi had gone upstairs to nap. Mama sat at the table while the aroma of cherry pie filled the house. Darn it. My greatest weakness was cherry pie.

Mama smiled at me and patted a hand on the table. She was up to something.

"Come, read Ellie Mae's articles."

I stiffened and frowned.

"Samuel."

My feet were smarter than I was. They took me to the table, so I sat down across from Mama. She pushed two pages towards me.

"Read it."

I turned over the first page. The headline said, "Governor Goodwin, Not the First Governor."

I read the article to myself and tried to keep a frown in place. It did no good. Ellie Mae told a captivating story about a doctor from Ohio who treated John A. Gurley, the first governor appointed by President Lincoln. She never mention-ed Mama's name. She only said that the young doctor and his wife ended up on the same wagon train as Governor Good-win.

"As fate would have it," I read out loud, "the young doctor who treated the first governor ended up passing away before he arrived in Prescott."

Mama's eyes teared up. She cleared her throat. "Only my closest friends and family will know this is about me and Drew."

I swallowed hard. It would be hard to stay angry with Ellie Mae after this.

"Read the next one."

I did. It was a very well-written and interesting article about Papa and his cowboys. That article was much longer as she covered the tales from the trip west and the early days setting up the ranch. I thought it was a wonderful piece. It put Papa in a very positive light. Those who respected him would respect him more. Strangers would think well of him.

"What did Papa think?"

76

Mama smiled. "He thinks they are great. He also thinks her editor might make her split up the article about him into two smaller ones. It seemed a little long."

"But it keeps the reader's attention," I defended.

Mama's smile grew wider. She reached across the table and squeezed my hand. "Do you want to talk about last night?"

I shook my head.

"Alright. If you ever do, you can talk to me or Will."

"I know."

"Why don't you go wash up? It is almost supper time, and you need to fetch Ellie Mae."

I stood and did what Mama asked. I knew I should apologize to Ellie Mae before supper. So that's what I did.

CHAPTER 13

ELLIE MAE

A knock sounded on my door. It surprised me to see Sam when I opened it as I did not expect him to walk me over to the house for supper.

"Hello." I was at a loss for words. I wondered if Hannah made him come or if he came of his own volition.

"Can I come in?" he asked.

"Let me grab my things and I'll join you outside shortly."

He nodded and stepped outside.

My heart danced in my chest. I put my notebook in my satchel and slung the strap over my arm. I placed the lamp on the table by the door and joined Sam outside.

He led me over to a large rock nearby. I leaned against it as he stood across from me.

He ran his hand through his hair. Then he paced back and forth in front of me. We might be late for supper if he did not get on with it soon.

"I'm sorry," he said, avoiding my gaze. He looked up as a bird squawked overhead. "I do not hate you. Sorry I said those things. I know I hurt you."

"Sam."

He looked at me then. I held out my hands. He waited several seconds before he took them.

"What my parents said shocked me. I was angry and con-fused and I took it out on you."

I held on to his hands even when he tried to pull them away.

"I can imagine," I said, "that it was very difficult to hear that someone had kidnapped you as a baby."

He looked at me then. "You don't hate me?"

I smiled and stood. I squeezed his hands. "It hurt me. But I could never hate you."

I wanted to step into his embrace, and I wanted him to kiss me. Instead, I dropped his hands and nodded toward the ranch house.

"We should probably head over for supper," I said.

"I'm really sorry," he said again as he offered his arm.

I took it and let out a slow breath.

"Are you sure you don't hate me?"

I laughed. "I don't make cherry pie for just anyone."

He stopped and turned toward me. "You made me a pie? After all that?"

"I wanted to make it really hard for you to stay angry with me."

He reached up and brushed his fingers across my cheek. I stopped breathing as fire trailed after his touch.

His voice was husky when he said, "You are something else, Ellie Mae."

Boone hollered from the porch. "Supper is getting cold!"

I smiled and started breathing again. Sam took my hand in his and we hurried into the house. All was forgiven.

Hannah smiled knowingly at me when she saw both of us smiling as we took our seats.

Sam held out my usual chair for me. Then he sat to my

right and Violet was on my left.

"Look," Violet whispered rather loudly. "There are the flowers I picked for you, Ellie Mae."

"Thank you," I whispered and bowed my head for the blessing.

I smiled as the rhythm of a Colter supper flowed. Not only was I falling for Sam, but I was also falling for his family. Three days went by fast. I would eventually have to move back to town. The thought stole my joy away as I wished I could stay longer.

Boone regaled the family with a dramatic account of the cliff he climbed that morning with his surveying equipment strapped to his back. No one noticed my demeanor changed. I was grateful. I did not want my mood to spoil the evening.

"We really liked your articles," Will said. "Split the second one into two before you take it to your editor."

"Thank you. I'll type that up tonight." I looked over at Sam.

"I liked the way you told the story about the first governor without revealing Mama's name."

I let out a long breath. It was very important to me that Sam approved of my articles, even more important than Will and Hannah's approval.

Deacon, Preston, and Boone were put out that they were not invited to read the articles. I promised they could read them after supper.

After everyone finished eating, Hannah made a big show of dessert. She cut a giant slice of cherry pie for Sam. Then she set it down in front of him.

"For you from Ellie Mae."

Sam's face and neck turned red. He smiled at me. I smiled back.

"No fair," Preston whined.

"Be patient, young man," Hannah said. She brought a piece of peach pie to Will. "For you from me."

Will caught her by the waist and pulled her close. Then he placed a hand on her neck and guided her lips toward his. It was a chaste kiss that brought a reaction from everyone at the table. Will grinned. Hannah's cheeks flushed. I smiled. Violet sighed. Sam's face turned redder. Boone rolled his eyes. Deacon snickered. Preston whined about not getting any pie.

I stood and helped Hannah dish up pie for the rest of the family. We even allowed Preston and Violet to have some of Sam's cherry pie since they wanted it.

I sat down and ate a bite of Hannah's peach pie. The crust melted in my mouth, and I was glad I used her recipe for Sam's pie.

He nudged my foot with his. "Tastes as good as Mama's pie."

I laughed. "Probably because I used her recipe, her dough, and her cherries."

"Yes, but you made it which was the hard part," Hannah said.

Sam whispered, "Thank you."

Warmth spread across my cheeks. It made me happy that he was happy.

"Hannah, do you know anyone else in the area that I could interview from the governor's wagon train?"

"Joshua Harrison was part of that train."

Will coughed. Hannah gave him a look. He quickly stuffed another bite of pie in his mouth.

"He was a lieutenant in the cavalry that traveled with our train. I think he also escorted the governor around the territory that first year."

"Do you think he would talk to me?"

"I'm sure. You will probably find him at his office. He owns the freight company, J.W. Harrison."

"Can I tell him you suggested I speak with him?"

Will shifted in his chair.

"Yes," Hannah answered. Then she turned to Will. "More pie?"

He cleared his throat. "No, thank you."

If I did not know better, there was a story behind Will's discomfort. I would not press it, though.

"Would I be able to borrow a horse tomorrow? My editor is expecting the articles. I also need to arrange the interview with Mr. Harrison."

"I can take you," Sam said. "Though, I'll need to work this evening since I'm behind."

"I can take you," Deacon volunteered. "Then Sam won't have to work tonight. I wanted to talk to the vet about working for him this fall."

Both Will and Hannah looked surprised by Deacon's announcement.

"When did you decide this?" Will asked.

"I was going to talk to you tonight. I've been reading a lot of the cattleman journals lately. Even though I've learned a lot from you, I want to study with the vet for a while and learn more about the latest advancements in animal husbandry."

I stood and helped Hannah clear the plates.

"Our family has been raising cattle the same way for generations," Will said.

"I know," Deacon said. "It doesn't hurt to learn about other things, does it? Maybe some advancements could help us keep the herd healthier or make birthing easier on the cows."

I glanced at Will while I cleared Preston's plate away. His mouth formed a thin line. His palms rested flat on the table. I don't know that I had seen Will angry, but I wondered if he might be.

"Let's talk out in the barn."

Boone, good old Boone, could not resist. "You're in trouble now, Deacon."

I found the whole thing amusing, so I hurried into the kitchen and started drawing water for the dishes. I figured none of the Colters found the exchange as funny as I did.

Hannah whispered, "I guess most of my boys are in that transition of becoming men. I think I should pray harder for Will. He doesn't like to be challenged, and it's going to require him to let them explore their own dreams."

Preston and Boone took my articles into the parlor. I heard Boone reading them out loud. Sam picked up some bills and ledgers from his desk and sat down at the table. Violet ran upstairs to get her book and then brought it downstairs to the parlor. Will and Deacon took their conversation outside to the barn.

After I finished the dishes, I took my articles and headed back to the cabin. When I stepped outside, Sam followed me.

"I'll walk you home."

"Thank you. I know I keep taking you away from your work."

"It's no trouble. I rather like walking with you."

He slid his hand down my arm to hold mine. I interlaced my fingers with his.

"I rather like walking with you, too."

"Since we still have a little sunlight left, you want to walk around the lake?"

"Alright."

He took my satchel from me and set it down in front of the cabin before he led me around the lake.

"Thank you for the pie. It was delicious."

Little flutters danced in my stomach. "You're welcome."

"I don't know how Papa's conversation with Deacon is going to go, but I'll take you into town tomorrow."

"I can ride by myself. You don't have to stop everything to take me."

"I know. I want to."

I smiled. I wanted him to take me, too.

"Ellie Mae?"

"Yes?"

"How long will you stay with us?"

To understand why that was important to him, I needed to see his face. I stopped and turned to him as I lightened the mood.

"Trying to get me out of your way?"

"No," he blurted. "Quite the opposite."

My pulse quickened as his eyes softened. He took my other hand in his.

"I would like to court you. I suppose I should write to your father or take a trip to see him to get his permission."

My lips suddenly felt parched, so I licked them. "You want to court me?"

What a crazy swing of the pendulum in one day. The previous night, he hated me. That night, he wanted to court me. My heart held on tight for the ride.

"Yes. Would you like that?"

"Yes."

He reached up and ran his fingers along my jawline. "Should I visit your father or write to him?"

"I…" My skin tingled where his fingers trailed a moment before, making it difficult to think. "You can write him. I will as well."

He smiled. "And what will you say?"

"That I met the most dependable man who makes me smile."

Sam laughed. "I like that. I should take you home now."

"Alright."

He turned and laced his fingers with mine, then walked me back to my cabin. I hoped he might kiss me, but he did not. His eyes lingered for a minute, though.

"Good night, Sam."

"Good night, Ellie Mae."

CHAPTER 14

June 10, 1887

SAM

On the day before my twenty-first birthday, the ranch settled into a new routine. Everyone, including myself, was used to Ellie Mae joining us for our meals. Many evenings, we listened to stories about the beginning of the ranch.

Every night when I walked her home, it got harder to say good night. She worked her way into my heart.

I knew asking to court her seemed rather fast. I had only known her for a few days. But I saw the way my brothers looked at her. They adored her too. If I moved slowly, one of them would certainly swoop in and try to win her heart. I had no intention of letting that happen.

In the back of my mind, I knew she would eventually leave the ranch. Though the thought saddened my heart, I had a letter to write. That letter was the key to solidifying my position with her.

Dear Mr. Thatcher,

My name is Samuel Colter. I am the second son of Will Colter of the Colter & Larson ranch. I make my living by managing the business side of the ranch, meat company, and training stables.

I am writing to you because I care for Ellie Mae and would like your permission to court her. You do not know me, which makes my request more difficult. I hope that Ellie Mae will write to you about my character. Also, Paul Lancaster is a long-time family friend who knows what kind of man...

I stopped. I was going to write, "what kind of man I am becoming." Most days, I still felt trapped between boyhood and manhood. My work was that of an adult. But inside, I still failed to see myself as a grown man.

I sighed loudly, which Mama heard from the kitchen.

"What is it, Sam?"

I ran a hand over my face.

"I'm writing to Ellie Mae's father."

That brought Mama to my side. "Oh?"

I had not told her about my intentions. Only Ellie Mae knew. I handed the incomplete letter to Mama, unable to say the words aloud.

Her eyes read the letter, then read my face. Then she smiled. "I think it is very good. I like how you acknowledged the difficulty of your request and how he might perceive it. That alone proves your character."

"I can picture what Papa might say if he received such a letter regarding Violet, when she is older, of course."

Mama nodded. "I think it might be nice for you to suggest a trip to meet her family in a few months. Give him an opportunity to meet you in person."

"Maybe I should travel now, instead of writing a letter. Ellie Mae should come with me so he could judge for himself."

Mama laid a hand on my shoulder. "I think the letter is

good. I would finish it and send it. Then suggest he visit the ranch, or you visit their farm."

"Thank you," I said.

She went back to the kitchen to finish whatever she was doing.

I finished the letter.

...what kind of man I am.

You and your family are welcome to visit our ranch if there is a convenient time. Or perhaps I could visit your farm to meet you, your wife, and your son.

Regards,

Samuel Colter

I sighed as I folded the letter and addressed the envelope. Lord, please help Mr. Thatcher to receive this letter with an open mind.

Ellie Mae entered the house. She spent the morning completing two more articles. One was about Adam's stables. When I read it, I was pleased. She wrote about the history of the stables and spoke highly of both Adam and Julia. I thought it might generate more business for him. The other was from her interview with Joshua Harrison.

When I finished reading the articles, I asked, "You ready to go into town?"

Before she answered, Mama dried her hands and joined us. "The whole family is going in today."

I held back a frown. I was looking forward to taking Ellie Mae to lunch alone.

"Tomorrow is Sam's birthday," Mama announced. "We need to do some shopping."

"Why didn't you say something?" Ellie Mae asked.

I shrugged. I did not mention it because, unlike Boone, I

did not like to draw attention to myself.

Her shoulders sagged, and her smile faded.

Boone burst through the door, followed by Deacon, Preston, and Papa. Violet set aside her book and entered the dining room with the rest of us.

"Ready?" Papa asked. "Wagon and horses are ready."

I sighed.

Papa helped Mama, Violet, and Ellie Mae up into the wagon. When I joined them, he pulled me aside.

"Boone is going to drive them. I'd like you to ride with me."

It was then I noticed Papa had his palomino gelding, Nug-get, saddled and tied next to Bailey. Deacon's blood bay gelding, Sergeant, and Preston's liver chestnut stallion, Ranger, were also saddled. I held back a smile at the thought of Boone driving the wagon. He'd rather ride his horse.

We mounted up. Preston and Deacon rode ahead of the wagon. Papa and I lagged. I grew nervous as I wondered what I did to prompt a talk.

"Your mother told me about the letter to Mr. Thatcher."

I swallowed hard.

"Why didn't you say something to us?" Papa looked at me. His expression was stony. "It hurt your mother."

Not only did I disappoint him again, I let down Mama too.

I bit the inside of my cheek. I was not sure my confident, secure father would understand.

"I worried you would be disappointed if Mr. Thatcher said no. The fewer people that knew, the less it would hurt when he rejects me."

Papa stopped Nugget and turned his horse so he could face me. "Sam, why do you think Mr. Thatcher would reject your request?"

I did not say reject my request. I said reject me. Papa did not think like me or notice the distinction. I was terrified that Mr. Thatcher would reject both.

"He doesn't know me."

"We can take a few days to meet Ellie Mae's family. Just say the word. I know as soon as he sees what a dependable, reliable young man you are, it would please him to let you court her."

Papa turned his horse back towards Prescott yet kept him close to Bailey.

"I'm a stranger asking him for his daughter. Would you be so calm if we were talking about Violet?"

Papa considered my words.

"You should not be so hard on yourself. You are a good man. Ellie Mae sees it. I'm sure her father will, too."

I kicked Bailey into a trot to catch up with the wagon, hoping to end the conversation.

Papa kept Nugget in pace with me. "Even though you did not ask our opinion, your mother and I are happy for you. We like Ellie Mae. She already feels like part of the family."

I held back a snort. Ellie Mae felt like she belonged in the family. I was the one that did not.

We caught up to the wagon, and I veered Bailey to the side where Ellie Mae sat. She smiled when I came up next to the wagon. It reminded me she was worth any rejection I might face.

Once we arrived in town, I tied Bailey to the hitching post near the mercantile. I helped Ellie Mae down from the wagon.

"I need to mail this letter to your father. Would you like to walk with me?" I asked.

"Of course."

"Do you have anything to mail?"

Ellie Mae smiled and put her hand in the crook of my arm. "I mailed a letter on Friday. I told him I hoped to become your sweetheart and that you are a good man."

I let out a long breath as we entered the post office. I paid for the postage and mailed the letter. Hopefully, her letter would arrive before mine and it was convincing.

"Relax. I'm sure Papa will respond quickly."

"Would you like to go to lunch?"

"I would love to."

I led her to Isabel's and, as fate would have it, we sat in front of the windows. No sooner did we sit down and order when I heard my name called.

I wanted to pretend I did not hear my brother. It was a terrible thought. But I was with Ellie Mae, and I was not ready for her to meet my older, better looking, more charming brother. I hoped to solidify a courtship before she ever met him.

"James." I turned to see him coming toward our table.

I saw his expression change the instant he saw Ellie Mae, and I did not like it. His dark brown eyes lit. His suave smile spread across his lips as he diverted his full attention to my woman.

When he reached out and took her hand, my spine stiffen-ed.

"Who is this lovely woman?" He took her hand and placed a kiss on top of it.

Her cheeks turned rosy, and I could not discern if it was from embarrassment or interest. I jerked forward slightly before I could stop myself.

"Ellie Mae, this is my older brother, James Colter. James, this is Miss Ellie Mae Thatcher." I wanted to say she was my sweetheart, but I only just mailed the letter to her father.

"Pleasure to meet you, Ellie Mae," James said, releasing her hand.

To my horror, James pulled out the chair next to mine and sat down. Then he got the server's attention and ordered a meal.

"Mr. Colter." Ellie Mae's voice was icy. "I don't recall either of us inviting you to take a seat."

I wanted to close my eyes and sink under the table. I appreciated she asserted herself. The problem was that she didn't know James. Her words prompted his competitive nature.

A grin spread across his lips slowly. His voice took on a saucy tone. "Come now, please call me James."

Our food arrived, and I felt trapped. That was not how I pictured lunch with Ellie Mae.

CHAPTER 15

ELLIE MAE

If only Sam could read my mind and ask his brother to leave. I saw him tense when James took my hand. He flinched with each slick word that dripped from James's silver tongue.

My mama warned me about men like James. She told me not to be fooled by their smooth words or charming smiles. Though the attention they lavished on a woman felt good, it did not last. There was no substance to a man like that.

When the server delivered our meal and Sam still did not act, I swallowed my disappointment before I took matters into my own hands.

"Would you mind boxing up mine?" I asked the server. She took my plate back to the kitchen.

"I'm sorry, Sam. It's late and I need to go. There is a meeting with my editor."

It pained me to crush his heart like that but I didn't want to spend more time with his brother.

"Editor?" James asked.

I ignored him.

The server brought my boxed meal, and I stood. Both

James and Sam stood. I took Sam's hand in mine and squeezed it.

"I will see you at supper," I whispered. "Thank you for lunch."

"I'm sorry," he whispered back.

Then I left without a farewell to his brother. I took my lunch and satchel and headed to the newspaper office.

I found a desk with my nameplate on it when I arrived, so I set my lunch on the desk. I let Clayton's secretary know I was in.

James's intrusion still infuriated me as I ate my lunch. The differences between Sam and his brother were obvious. They both had the same dark brown hair. Sam's eyes were that mesmerizing shade of blue, where James's eyes were dark brown. James was shorter than Sam by several inches. In fact, he was closer to my height than Sam's. They both dressed in modern tailored suits, but James had more flash about him. He wore a silk neck scarf and carried an expensive looking dark wood walking stick with a polished brass handle.

Where Sam was reserved, James was brash. He was too forward with me. He showed no regard for his brother. Even if his words flattered or tempted me, his dismissal of Sam killed any further consideration before it rooted.

I opened my satchel and pulled out my draft articles while I waited for my editor. Then I wrote the beginning of another article by hand. I missed my typewriter.

"Ellie Mae," Clayton greeted me. "I see you found your desk. How do you like it?"

I smiled. "It's nice."

He raised an eyebrow. "But?"

"I may need to bring my typewriter. I'm spoiled writing with it now."

He laughed. "If you want to bring it in, you can. Do you have a few minutes?"

I nodded, and he motioned me to his office.

When I took a seat across from him, he started, "The response to the Prescott Pioneers series is extremely positive. Folks like your writing style and your perspective."

My cheeks warmed under the praise. "Thank you."

"How much longer will you stay at the Colters?"

My stomach tightened. I knew I could not stay there much longer. "I finished interviewing everyone I intended to."

"Excellent. Can you move back into town on Monday?"

"I suppose so."

Clayton smiled. "I have several assignments for you in town that are not related to the Pioneers series. First, I need you to interview the management at the Central Arizona Railway. I understand James Colter works there. Have you met him?"

I hesitated, as my gut told me that my editor's next request would upset me. "Only just. I ran into him at Isabel's and Sam introduced me."

"Good. I'll have my secretary set up a time for you to meet with him early next week to learn more about the issues with the tracks. I've heard a rumor that there are concerns about the materials. The way they constructed the roadbed caused delays in the train."

"Alright."

"See if he can introduce you to Thomas Bullock, the President of the company. I would like you to press them about when they will complete a roundhouse. It's ridiculous that the train drives all the way from Prescott to Seligman in reverse. You can interview some passengers and take the trip yourself."

My heart picked up pace. He was giving me a real investigative piece.

"The newspaper will cover the cost of your fare and hotel in Seligman."

Then Clayton frowned. "I've heard rumors that Seligman is a little rough. Can Colter go with you as a guide? It might be safer than traveling alone as a woman."

When he first said Colter, I immediately thought of Sam. Then I realized he meant the railroad Colter brother. I held back a cringe.

I understood what a tremendous opportunity Clayton presented to me, a woman journalist. An exclusive interview on the conditions of the fledgling railroad was a coup.

"Are you looking for multiple stories?" I asked as the possibilities formed in my mind.

Clayton smiled. "You have good instincts, Thatcher. Let's see what you dig up. If it leads to multiple articles, then all the better."

"I'll start drafting some questions today." I stood and returned to my desk as anticipation flooded my soul.

For the next few hours, I researched the background of the Central Arizona Railway, the board members, and the management staff. I took copious notes and questions formed in my mind. I lost track of time.

"Ellie Mae."

I looked up at the sound of Sam's voice.

"Are you coming back to the ranch today?" Sadness coated his words.

"Yes." I looked at my watch pin. It was after four o'clock. I stuffed my things in my satchel and stood. "I'm so sorry."

"My family left hours ago. Papa left his horse for you. Can you ride astride?" His face turned red as he asked the quest-ion.

"I never have, but I suppose I can try it."

He frowned. "I'll leave my saddle at the livery and rent you a sidesaddle. Papa would not be pleased if I came home without his saddle."

"It's alright, Sam. I will figure it out."

He led me out front to where the horses waited.

"The last thing I would want is for you to fall from a horse."

He led me and the horses to Thomas Anderson's livery. Thomas agreed to store Sam's saddle until he returned early next week. I had yet to tell him I would move back to town on Monday. It bothered me he would be without his saddle.

"You can ride Bailey. He's gentler than Papa's horse."

Sam placed the sidesaddle on Bailey's back. Then he gave me a leg up. He mounted Nugget and led us out of town.

His mind ruminated over something. I could see it. That was Sam. A thinker. It made me feel even more special that he asked to court me. He did not come to that decision lightly.

"How fast is Bailey?" Suddenly, I was in the mood to be impulsive.

"Fast enough. Why?"

"Race ya!" I kicked Bailey into a gallop. It took a few sec-onds before I heard fast hoofbeats behind me.

I leaned closer to Bailey's neck. He was a powerful horse, like the strong man chasing me. The wind in my face delighted me as the smooth gait of the horse beneath me brought joy to my heart. We moved as one.

After a few miles, I slowed Bailey to a trot. Sam and Nug-get were right beside me.

As I placed a hand on my hat, I laughed and looked at

Sam. His brilliant blue eyes gleamed in the late afternoon light as his cheeks flushed. As if coaxing a smile from him was not enough of a treasure, he laughed a soul-deep laugh, which brought a thrilling shiver to my skin.

When his laughter faded, his eyes surveyed my face, lips, and eyes.

"You fill my soul with joy, Ellie Mae."

My mouth went dry as I unconsciously touched a hand to my neck. If we had not been on horseback, he would have kissed me. Everything about his gaze spoke he wanted to.

It was going to be impossible to tell him I was leaving.

CHAPTER 16

SAM

James chuckled as Ellie Mae left. He moved his plate to where she had sat a moment ago. Then he took her seat. I frowned and tried to stop thinking about punching his arrogant face.

"She said she's on her way to her editor. Is she a writer?" James asked.

I took a stealthy, deep breath. Then I let it out, so our meal would remain civilized.

"She's a journalist." I took a bite of my food and chewed it slowly, not offering more information than that.

"What newspaper?"

"The Prescott Gazette."

James took a bite of his food. "I don't recall any women reporters there."

"She uses her initials."

"E. M. Thatcher? She's E. M.?" James's eyes grew wide.

"Yes."

James snorted. "Who knew? E. M. is a woman. I've read her series. I liked what she wrote about Father and the ranch."

I focused on my meal. The less I said to him, the better.

"She's a beauty, even if she does dress rather plainly."

I stopped chewing and glared at him.

He laughed. "You like her? Never saw that coming."

My eyes shot bullets in his direction.

"Why are you here?" I asked through clenched teeth.

"As I was on my way to my office, I saw you and I was hungry. I already ran into the family at the mercantile, so it surprised me to see you eating lunch without them. Then I saw her."

He studied me for a good minute.

"I also wanted to talk to you about investing in the Central Arizona Railroad."

As he changed the topic, I stopped glaring despite my dis-taste of the new one.

"You know my thoughts on the matter."

"The railroad is the way of the future."

I could practically recite his speech as it changed little over the years.

"It's a solid investment. Our line runs from Prescott to Seligman. We're the only feeder line to the Atlantic & Pacific."

I took a sip of my iced tea and kept my face impassive.

"You could grow the ranch more by shipping cattle east or even west to California."

"Shouldn't you talk to Papa about it?"

"Father listens to you. If you think it is a good idea, then he'll follow your lead."

"Papa is his own man. He owns the majority stake in the ranch. If he doesn't want to do it, he won't, regardless of what I say."

James frowned. "He will if you're on board with the idea."

"I share his concerns. It is just a matter of time before

your line, or another, crosses our land and splits our grazing grounds in half. How are we supposed to manage a herd waiting for a train to pass?"

"We aren't building a line through Colter property. I won't let that happen."

I snorted. "You think you really have the power to stop it?"

"If you were investors, I would have more leverage."

I failed to take the bait of his new tactic. "I'm gonna pass."

His leg bobbed up and down under the table, causing my iced tea to slosh up the sides of the glass. "Look, would you consider doing it to support me?"

"Are you in some kind of trouble?"

His leg stopped moving as his salesman persona returned. "No. No."

I nodded to the server to get the check. "I still need to head out to Fort Whipple today."

I paid for my meal and Ellie Mae's. James could pay for his own. Then I stood.

"See you at the ranch tomorrow?"

He smiled. "You know I wouldn't miss your birthday."

I nodded and left.

As I mounted Bailey and pointed him toward the fort, my mind stewed over James's unusual behavior. I understood him goading me about Ellie Mae. That was his way.

His persistence frustrated me, and I would not invest in his railroad. I heard rumblings from some of our customers about their negative experiences with the train. That alone kept me from investing in it. James and his bosses needed to work out some kinks.

I kicked Bailey into a trot to get to the fort quicker. Once there, I met with the supply officer to collect payment for previous orders. Then I confirmed his order for the next few weeks.

By the time I arrived back in town, my family sat waiting in the wagon.

"Where's Ellie Mae?" Papa asked.

"She went to the Gazette to work."

Papa nodded toward Nugget. "I'll leave him for her. You'll both be home for supper?"

"Yes, sir."

Papa took a seat on the wagon next to Mama. Boone sat in the back with Violet. He frowned. I smiled. I imagined if Deacon and Preston were still there, he would have swindled one of them out of their horse. It would do him good to sit in the wagon for a ride home.

I stopped at several other customers to take payment and confirm upcoming orders. When Ellie Mae had not found me by four o'clock, I went in search of her.

When I entered the newspaper office, the smell of musty paper and ink filled the room. It made my nose twitch. A small desk stood at the front. Behind the counter, they spaced eight desks evenly throughout the office. Large file cabinets lined the back wall. To my left, was an office and library. Files lined the side of the office.

On the right, someone opened a door. The smell of ink overpowered the space. Noise filled the room until the door closed.

I greeted the receptionist and asked for Ellie Mae. He pointed over his shoulder at her desk and let me in.

For a few minutes, I watched her. She bit her lower lip as she read a piece of paper. Then she wrote some notes in her journal. She narrowed her eyes and frowned. Then she tapped her pencil on the page before furiously scribbling in her journal.

When she set her pencil down and sat straighter, I greeted her.

She smiled. "Sam."

I loved the way she said my name. It was like the sunlight on an early spring day, warm and inviting after standing in the cool shadows for too long.

She gathered her things and walked with me to the horses.

It pained me to leave my saddle behind. Papa's voice scolded me in my head. A man doesn't leave his saddle. The greater offense would be to force Ellie Mae to ride astride.

When we were outside of the city limits, Ellie Mae's face lit with excitement.

"Race ya!"

Before my mind processed her words, she took off at a full gallop on my horse. I kicked Nugget, and he leaped forward to match Bailey's pace. Her riding skill was obvious in her graceful movements which paralleled Bailey's strides.

When she slowed Bailey's pace, I pulled up next to her. My heart overflowed, and I laughed. I said something profound, then I searched her gaze. Never had I wanted to kiss her more than in that moment.

The joy in her eyes told me I had nothing to worry about. She was my woman. What she saw in me, I did not know. But she was mine.

I hoped I would not let her down.

"We should probably not delay," I said at length. "Mama will have supper ready soon."

When we crested the last hill before the ranch, I spotted a man leading a sable-colored horse into the barn. I recognized the horse; he was Brass, and he belonged to James.

My jaw tightened. I hoped he would wait until tomorrow to make the trip out.

"What is it?" Ellie Mae asked.

I schooled my features. "James is here."

"Oh."

I gathered she was about as excited as a rock by her tone. I held back a smile. That was my girl.

After we pulled up in front of the barn, I dismounted from my horse before I helped Ellie Mae down. My hands lingered on her waist as she smiled up at me. Then she surprised both of us when she placed a kiss on my cheek.

"Remember, I won that race," she teased. "See you in a few minutes."

She squirmed out of my hold, grabbed her satchel, and walked toward her cabin.

"Are you courting her?" James's voice eradicated all the warm feelings I relished a moment earlier.

Even though I wanted to, I would not consider it until I heard from her father. Neither did I want to encourage my brother.

"A lot of things have changed."

I led the horses into the stable. He took Nugget's reins and led him to his stall while I took care of Bailey.

"If she's your woman, then claim her," James said.

It took every ounce of self-control not to clobber him.

"What does it matter to you?"

James said nothing more.

Until we entered the house. Ellie Mae waited for me at the foot of the table. I held her chair and then sat down next to her as usual. Vi sat down when James moved behind that chair.

"Scoot over, Vi."

"But I always sit next to Ellie Mae," Vi whined.

Papa must have seen my jaw twitching from the other end of the table. "James, pick a different chair."

James narrowed his eyes at Papa.

Papa stood. The two of them stared off like a gunfight at high noon.

"Vi, go ahead and take the seat," Papa said calmly.

Her chair scraped against the floor and echoed in the silence. James moved to the other side of the table and sat next to me. Papa sat down.

"Deacon, will you say grace for us tonight?"

Papa still stared down James as I bowed my head. While Deacon prayed, I wondered if either of them did.

"Amen," the rest of us parroted after Deacon said it.

The tension between Papa and James eased. Not so for my feelings toward my brother. I hated he sat next to me. He would be in Ellie Mae's line of sight every time she looked at me which was probably his aim. I wished I could get away with trading spots with Violet.

CHAPTER 17

ELLIE MAE

James's presence added tension to the meal. I, for one, did not like it. I could tell Sam was none too pleased, either.

"Ms. Thatcher, my secretary tells me I have an interview with you on Tuesday."

I glanced at Sam. He frowned.

"Yes. My editor asked me to write a piece about your railroad."

"Oh, that's good news!" Hannah exclaimed.

I smiled. "Yes. My pioneers' articles are popular, so he wants to challenge me with a different type of article."

James held my gaze. Even though he fished for more details, he would get nothing from me.

"He said that I would escort you to Seligman on Wednesday and back on Thursday."

I glared at him. I didn't want Sam to hear the news from someone else.

"Is it true?" Sam's voice held a hint of hurt.

Looking directly at him, I said, "It was my plan to talk to you after supper. I would still like to."

James noticed when Sam reached for my hand.

I spoke before James could say anything else. "My editor

thought if I rode the train, I could write about the experience firsthand."

"I can give you a behind-the-scenes tour of the station in Seligman, if you'd like," James said.

Sam stiffened, so I simply thanked James for the offer.

Soon enough, Hannah changed the topic, and the friction between Sam and James diminished. I breathed easier as well.

As soon as supper finished, James tried to capture my attention again.

"There is still plenty of sunlight left. Would you care for a stroll around the lake?" James asked.

"Oh, that is a wonderful idea. Thank you for suggesting it to Sam and me. Sam, shall we?"

James scowled, and Sam offered me his arm.

When we were outside, he gave me some advice. "Be careful with James. When he doesn't get what he wants, he can be a cad."

"I want to make it clear to him that my heart belongs to you," I whispered.

Sam smiled down at me and put his hand over mine. "Thank you. All the same, be careful. This is uncharted territory in the Colter family. I don't know the motivation behind his behavior. I don't like it."

We walked in silence. At the halfway mark, I stopped.

"Sam." I sighed. "My editor wants me to move back to town."

He stood in front of me. "When?"

"Monday." My heart ached as he ran a hand through his hair.

"So soon?" He put his hand in mine.

"I've been here a week and a half, and I've completed my interviews." I lowered my gaze, then I looked up at him.

"That is why I came here, remember?"

He sighed. "I don't have to like it, do I?"

My pulse raced. I placed my hand on his cheek. "No, you don't. I will miss you."

He moved his head, so his lips pressed against the palm of my hand. "I can't remember what the ranch was like before you arrived."

When he said things like that, my heart bonded tighter to his. I loved Sam Colter and I would miss him terribly.

I moved closer and wrapped my arms around his middle. I rested my head against his chest as he caressed my back. We stood there as the sun inched lower in the sky.

"You fill my soul with joy," I murmured.

"What's that?" he asked.

I looked up at him. "Just something you said to me after I raced your horse. You fill my soul with joy."

"You do," he whispered.

He traced his finger along my neck. "I really want to kiss you."

"Then kiss me." I wanted him to.

He groaned. "I want to wait for your father's permission to court you. But you are making it very difficult."

I stepped back and smiled. "*I* am making it difficult?"

He took my hand and interwove his fingers with mine. Then he tugged, and I fell into step beside him as he walked me toward my cabin. "You are. You look at me with those big nutmeg eyes of yours as if I was your entire world."

You are. I thought.

"I could lose myself in those eyes, Ellie Mae."

I understood what he meant. I felt like the only woman in the world when I looked into his blue eyes.

When we rounded the corner of the trail, he stopped. "You didn't say, but I got the feeling you wanted to go home."

"Yes. I need to write."

He leaned down and kissed my cheek. "Good night, Ellie Mae."

"Good night, Sam."

I stood outside the door and watched as he headed down the path to his house. When he stepped into the shadow of the porch, I turned and went inside.

As the sun hid behind the horizon, I lit a lamp. I opened my personal journal and wrote the three special things he said to me that day. I filled his soul with joy. He could not remember life at the ranch before me. He could lose himself in my eyes. For a quiet man who rationed words, when he spoke them, they were worth hearing.

After a few minutes, I sat down at my typewriter. His birthday was tomorrow, and I wanted to give him the gift of my words. My mind mulled over the words I wanted to say. I weighed the choice of each word. Then I typed a love note to my man.

I decided not to address it or to sign it. I would give it to him on his birthday with the other gifts from his family. It was clear they were my words to him. Should he ever doubt his position in my heart, he would always have those words typed on a piece of paper to remind him.

As I reread the words, it occurred to me that regardless of what my father said, Sam and I were most definitely courting. I would honor Sam's decision to wait for a letter from my father before confirming it with spoken words.

I folded the paper in half and set it aside on the table. Then I turned my attention to my novel. My heroine needed to say a few things to her hero.

After another hour, I set my manuscript aside and readied for bed. I reread my note to Sam, satisfied with what I wrote. Then I went to bed and dreamed of my future with my hero.

CHAPTER 18

SAM

It was my twenty-first birthday, and I should have been happy, but two things weighed heavily on my mind. The first was Ellie Mae's move back to town. The second was her railroad trip.

I woke early. Boone still snored. Light barely streamed through the window. I dressed and went downstairs to a quiet house. Even Mama was not up yet.

I started a fire in the stove and fixed a pot of coffee. When it was ready, I poured a cup and went out onto the front porch. I sat in a rocker and watched the sun rise.

"Sam?" Mama whispered from the doorway.

"Morning."

She carried a cup of coffee and sat in the rocker next to me. "Why are you up so early?"

"Mama, can I ask you a favor?"

"Of course."

"Will you go on the train with Ellie Mae?" I did not meet her gaze. I could feel it penetrating the profile of my face.

"I would enjoy riding on a train. I have never done that," she conceded. "Why do you want me to?"

I told Mama everything about my exchange with James at the restaurant.

"I can't decide if he is acting strange because he wants to make me jealous or if he is interested in her or if it is something else entirely. All I know is that I don't feel comfortable with her being alone with him for hours or overnight."

I angled to look at her then.

She rocked the chair slowly, so she did not spill her coffee. She took a few sips. "Alright. I will ask James to pay for my ticket and room. My motives will be pure, since I would like to learn about his job."

She winked at me.

"And you're right. He has been acting strangely. He won't step out of line with me there."

I stood and helped Mama to her feet. Then I kissed her cheek.

"Thank you, Mama."

She patted a hand on my cheek. "Happy Birthday, Sam."

I smiled as she turned and went back inside. It was the biggest favor I asked from her.

I sat down in the rocking chair and sipped my coffee until it was gone. I would miss Ellie Mae, but it was probably good that we spent some time apart. We grew close so quickly, partly because we spent so much time together. A little distance would not hurt us, as long as she did not forget about me.

A movement near her cabin caught my attention. She stepped out of the cabin with her long brown hair loose. She wore a blue dress. The light breeze caught her hair, obscuring her view. She tripped and fell.

I smiled. That woman spent more time on her backside. I resisted the temptation to run to her and help her up. I doubted she knew anyone was awake or out of the house yet.

She stood and smoothed out her skirt before she picked up the pail. Then she turned the corner out of sight, headed to the water pump. When she appeared again, she stopped and raised a hand to shade her eyes. Even though she was some distance away, I could tell she smiled. She waved.

I waved back.

Then she disappeared inside. A few minutes later, she came back out with her hair coiled at the base of her neck. She headed down the path toward me.

"Morning," Ellie Mae said softly when she was within ear-shot. "You're up early."

"Care for some coffee?"

She nodded, and I went inside to fetch her a cup and re-fill my own. Then I took a seat in my rocker. She sat next to me.

"Just thinking about you this morning. I'm going to miss seeing you every day. And walking with you."

She reached over and squeezed my hand. "I'll miss you, too. But I need to do this."

"I understand." I wished she could stay at the ranch long-er.

"We better get inside for breakfast," she said.

I stood and escorted her inside.

The rest of the morning flew by with routine ranch work. After lunch, my brothers cornered me outside.

"When are we going to practice for the big game?" Boone asked.

Deacon added, "We've only got three weeks before the In-dependence Day celebration. Normally, we've started practicing by now."

Boone tossed me a baseball and my mitt.

"Not to worry, brothers," James said. "The distraction of

a woman will not make Sammy a bad pitcher."

I frowned, growing weary of James's jabs.

Preston arrived in the side yard with Uncle Adam, Aunt Julia, Penny, and Dory. The girls wore trousers. Mama, Papa, Vi, and Ellie Mae joined them. When several cowboys rode in from the herd, I surmised a conspiracy was afoot.

I followed my family out to the nearest pasture. My brothers already marked lines for the baseball diamond and sacks of feed for the bases.

"Every year," Mama explained to Ellie Mae, "We play baseball at the town's Independence Day celebration. It's Colter & Larson Ranch against the town businessmen. The girls don't get to play in the actual game, but they help with practice. Sam is our pitcher."

"I think I will sit out," Ellie Mae said.

"That's fine. You can share a blanket with us and cheer them on."

I helped Ellie Mae take a seat next to Mama. When my brothers got too rowdy, I stepped up to the pitcher's mound.

I threw a few balls toward Papa at home plate to warm up. Then, we divided into two teams. I usually pitched for both teams during our practices.

"Play ball!" Aunt Julia called as she was first up to bat.

I knew better than to go easy on her or her daughters. She would take me to task if I did.

So, I planted my right leg perpendicular to the home plate. Then I lifted my left leg while I brought my right arm up over my head. At just the right moment, I released the ball, and it sped toward Aunt Julia. She flinched but did not swing, and Papa called it a strike.

My second pitch was perfect. Aunt Julia swung and connected with the ball for a single base. She was great at every sport she ever tried.

Boone was up next. Preston and I secretly practiced pitching a curve ball in the spring before Ellie Mae came to the ranch. I learned it specifically to make Boone's game more challenging.

It worked. He swung and missed.

"What the heck was that?" Boone's face went red.

I smiled. "A legal ball that you missed."

He wasn't used to missing.

"Want me to try it again? See if you can hit it."

He grunted and took his stance again.

I threw another curve ball. He tipped it for a fowl.

On the third curve ball, he made contact. The ball landed in the outfield. It was a home run. After he tagged home plate, he came up to me.

"What was that for?" Boone frowned.

"You needed the practice. I heard a rumor that Leroy Jen-kins was learning the curve ball just for you. So, this is good practice. Just watching your back, is all."

Boone's frown disappeared, and he slapped me hard on my back. "Good, we'll show Leroy there ain't nothing I can't hit."

I smiled despite the stinging skin on my back. Boone did nothing in half measure.

We played for a few hours, even after Mama, Vi, and Ellie Mae left to start supper. My arm was sore. My brothers were right. I should have practiced with them in the evenings. That would be easier to do with Ellie Mae moving to town on Monday.

"See," I teased them as we headed back towards the house. "Nothing to worry about. I still have the fastest ball in the west."

"You should hit each of us with that curve ball next

week," Deacon suggested. "No telling when Leroy might use it on any of us."

"Alright."

As we neared the lake, Boone veered toward it, stripped off all his clothes and dove in. When he came up for air, he hollered to the rest of us.

"Come on in, boys!"

I continued to the house, embarrassed by his lack of couth. Thankfully, Julia and her girls were far ahead of us. The rest of my brothers, including James, followed his lead. So did the cowboys.

I popped my head into the kitchen to warn Mama and Ellie Mae. "Avoid looking out any windows facing the lake. The boys are swimming Boone-style."

I heard Ellie Mae ask Mama what that meant. Better that she explained it.

Stepping back outside, I went over to the water pump and pumped a bucket of fresh water. I took off my shirt and washed up. Then I rinsed my hair with the rest of the water. When I finished, I put my shirt back on.

"Boys!" Mama's voice carried across the lawn. "Supper is almost ready!"

None of my brothers heard, so I headed that way to gather them. It took a few minutes to get them moving. They were still fairly wet when they put their clothes back on.

We entered the house, and Ellie Mae broke out in a fit of laughter. "You look like a bunch of drowned rats! This will be a scene in my novel. I'll work it in."

Boone was the only one that showed no embarrassment. He grinned as if she paid him a compliment.

She came over and placed a kiss on my cheek. Then she combed her fingers through my hair. "That's better."

120

I caught her waist when she tried to move away. For the first time, I ignored our audience.

"Am I in your novel?" I asked.

Her cheeks bloomed bright red. "Not directly."

"You'll let me read it one day, right?"

She nodded and escaped my hold. Then she stood by her usual chair. I held it out for her and took my seat.

At supper, Mama found a brilliant way of inviting herself on the train trip.

"James, I would love to take a few days off to come see your railroad line." She smiled sweetly across the table at him.

"You would?" James asked with wide eyes.

"Of course. You've talked about the railroad for years. It is about time you take your mama on a trip."

Preston perked up. "I'd like to go too."

Mama rested her hand on Preston's shoulder. "Perhaps another time. I'd like to spend the time with James. Well, and Ellie Mae too. It would be fun to watch a journalist in the field."

Papa cleared his throat. "We can manage for a day or two without you, but we might starve if you're gone longer."

Mama laughed at Papa's teasing. Then she held his gaze. "I'll miss you too."

"But, not to worry," Mama added. "Cousin Penny agreed to handle meals for you while I'm gone."

It occurred to me that Mama made all the plans without waiting for James to agree. I saw where James got his persuasiveness from. It was Mama. I hid my smile behind my hand.

At length, he finally said, "Mama, I would love to treat you to a ride on the railway. I'll cover your hotel in Seligman as well. I'll have my secretary get you and Ellie Mae rooms close together."

"Thank you, James. I'm really looking forward to it."

Just like that, any worries I had about Ellie Mae riding the train with James vanished.

CHAPTER 19

SAM

After supper, we gathered in the parlor for my birthday. They made me sit in the chair closest to the fireplace as each one presented me with a gift. Preston, Deacon, and Boone went together on a new baseball mitt. James got me a blue neck scarf. I would probably only wear it on Sundays to church. It was a little fancy for my taste, but I appreciated the gift. Violet got me a dime novel.

Mama and Papa asked Ellie Mae to go next. She stood and crossed the room. Then she handed me a paper.

She whispered so only I could hear, "These words are for your eyes only."

She held my gaze as I took the paper. Then she sat down and watched me with great interest as I unfolded the paper. I read the words silently.

> From the moment you first helped me down from a horse, I fell deep into your brilliant blue eyes. You said nothing with words, only with your eyes. I knew you found my appearance pleasing, and it stirred something in me.

I swallowed hard. She felt something that first day, too. It warmed my heart.

Then as one day became two and two became three, I

learned how rich your heart is. You ration words and smiles to such a degree that when I am graced with either, I accept them for the treasures that they are. I write them in my journal to remind my heart of the gift you gave me. I will savor them while we are apart.

I glanced up at her and held her gaze for several seconds. She smiled. I looked down to finish reading.

Three days became four. Four rolled into a week. A week grew into more.

You said that I bring joy to your soul. You bring joy to mine.

I look at you as if you are my world because you are. You are my heart, my breath, my world. My eyes see only you. My heart beats in rhythm with yours. 'You' and 'I' ceased to be. Now there is only 'we.'

I blinked as my eyes stung a little. Gone was any doubt that she loved me. She said it with so many words without saying it at all. Ellie Mae Thatcher loved me. She loved me for the man I was.

I coughed to mask the emotion welling inside of me so I could finish reading the words.

I don't know what the coming weeks apart will bring, but I know this: I long to be near you again, to hear your voice, to read the words in your eyes, and to feel the warmth of your smile.

Happy Birthday, my man, my heart, my soul.

My eyes found hers again. She could read my eyes. She knew I loved her. No words were necessary.

Boone snatched the paper from my hands.

"Boone." Ellie Mae said assertively, without raising her voice or taking her eyes away from mine. "Those words are for Sam and Sam alone."

Then she looked at him. "Do not betray my trust."

Boone handed the paper back to me and sat down. I folded the paper and put it in my shirt pocket close to my heart.

In that moment, my heart knew she would become my wife one day. I would wait patiently for her father to write back and for a little more time to pass.

Papa cleared his throat. I turned my attention to him and Mama.

"I guess this is the year of paper gifts, son. Though I have nothing to give you tonight."

He stood and walked over to me. I stood beside him as he addressed the family. He placed a hand on my shoulder and gave it a squeeze.

"As you have seen over the last few years, Sam manages this ranch. As I give him more responsibility, he rises to the occasion."

Pride welled inside of me.

Then he turned to me. "Your mama and I have decided it is time to give you a stake in Colter & Larson Ranch. On Mon-day, we'll meet with the attorney to draw up the paperwork. You will be a twenty percent owner of the business."

My brothers whispered among themselves, but Papa shut them down.

"I will only make ownership in this ranch available to those of you who stay and work for it."

"Your mother and I would like to see each of you pursue your dreams. James is doing that with the railroad, and he earns a fine wage for it. Boone, you are doing well surveying. I can't see you wanting to help run the ranch, but if you did, we would offer you a stake."

"Deacon, Preston, you are still figuring out your dreams. But, know this: if you choose to work at the ranch, we will offer you a stake."

"I saw firsthand what dividing a ranch between brothers can do. My brother and I were at odds. The only way to resolve it was to split the ranch in two after my father died. I will not have this ranch suffer the same fate. It goes to those who commit to it and to no one else."

He turned and looked at me. "You have proven your commitment to this ranch repeatedly. So, you've earned a stake. If your brothers choose to pursue their own paths, then one day, the entire place will be yours."

I could hardly breathe. It was such an extravagant gift. I did not feel worthy of it.

Papa lowered his voice. "You deserve this, Sam. You have earned it and you are worthy of it."

My eyes burned as Papa pulled me into a long bear hug. Maybe I wasn't a disappointment after all.

CHAPTER 20

ELLIE MAE

Sam would remember his twenty-first birthday for years to come. Between my note to him and his papa's gift of the ranch, nothing would ever top that.

When his father finally released him from a hug, Sam went over to his mama and hugged her as well. The scene was so touching. I was glad to be a part of it.

Hannah's eyes were red when she pulled away. She smiled as she dabbed at them.

"Let's have some cake!" she said.

Violet and I followed her to the kitchen to help as the men congratulated Sam. Mostly, his brothers accepted their par-ents' decision. Boone was the only moody one about the whole thing. Probably had less to do with the ranch and more to do with some gap he perceived in his relationship with one of his parents.

Deacon and James seemed the most accepting. James was relieved to have no ties to the ranch. From supper time conversations over the past two weeks, it sounded like Dea-con wanted to pursue veterinary medicine or something similar. The two of them had other career plans.

We left the parlor and sat at the table. I gave Sam a piece

of cake. Then I placed a hand on his shoulder. "Happy birth-day."

He cleared his throat. "Thank you."

Hannah and I served the others, then took our seats. The table was unusually quiet as everyone ate cake. When eve-ry-one was done, they all congratulated Sam again before they returned to the parlor.

Sam pulled me aside.

"Sit with me on the porch?" he asked. He took my hand when I nodded.

He angled one of the rocking chairs to get a better view of me. Then he sat. He took out my note and unfolded it. Then he read it again, slowly, as if he savored every word.

"Do you really mean this?" he asked.

"Of course, I do."

He swallowed several times.

"You don't need to say anything," I whispered.

"But I think I do. Such words deserve a response." His voice was husky.

My pulse raced as I realized my words touched him even deeper than I thought. I wanted to take the paper back and reread what I wrote.

He cleared his throat. "Most of my life, I felt like a misfit. Like I don't belong in my family and that I am not a part of anything."

My heart ached for him.

"That I am not worthy of anyone's love or affection. This perplexes me. Maybe it's related to the kidnapping. Maybe not."

He reached for my hand, and I gave it freely.

"Ellie Mae, seeing myself through your eyes encourages me. I see good things about myself that I never saw before. It makes me feel more worthy of your love."

I smiled.

Then he stood and drew me into his arms. His eyes searched mine. My breath shallowed as I read a deep abiding love there.

"You see me now as the man that I hope to one day become."

Then he lowered his head and gave me the briefest of kiss-es. Yet he communicated a thousand words with it. He would fight for me, care for me, and never leave me.

"Be patient with me," he said. "I would like to kiss you, leaving no question in your mind about how I feel. Except I want to show your father the respect and honor that he deserves, and wait for his response, even if it means I move at a slower pace with you."

Oh, how I loved that man! How could I not grant him that?

I rested my head against his chest to lessen the longing for a deeper kiss yet remain close.

We stood there for a long time. The sun lowered in the sky as we lingered in the embrace.

"Thank you, Sam."

He pulled away. "For what?"

"For supporting my dream of writing. You never complained about it, even though it is taking me away from you for a time."

He placed a hand on my cheek. "Of course. You and your dream are intertwined. I could not love you if I resented your desire to be a journalist."

I laughed. "You always say the right thing to me."

His eyes glinted in the fading light. "I suppose that comes with being my mama's boy."

That brought a heartier laugh from me. He joined in.

"It's been a long day. Walk me home?"

He did. As I watched him walk away, my pride for him grew. I was happy his parents were giving him the ranch.

A tear trickled down my cheek. I would miss seeing him every day.

CHAPTER 21

SAM

On Sunday afternoon, when Ellie Mae was at the house, I took the typewriter crate to the cabin. Deacon watched for her to alert me if she headed that way. I had a note to type before packing up her machine.

I followed her pattern, no address, and no signature. That made it seem even more personal. I would always know the note was from her. So, I would return her the favor.

> Your words to me on my birthday have bonded my heart to yours in ways I cannot describe. I have read and reread them so many times that I nearly have them memorized.
>
> Your smile is brighter than sunlight itself. Your laughter is like a bird's song in spring. It holds joy and promise, and it lifts my spirits instantly.
>
> Be safe, my love, in your travels. Know that you are in my prayers daily. I long for the day when we will never be apart.

They were bold words, but they were true. I would not hide them from her any longer.

I folded the piece of paper in my pocket to give to her

to-morrow as she moved into town.

Then I packed up her typewriter and left her cabin. It was no longer Grandpa Ben's cabin. It was Ellie Mae's. Every time I saw it, I would think of her.

The rest of Sunday flew by. Mama, Vi, and Ellie Mae watched the rest of us play another game of baseball. We had supper. Then I walked with Ellie Mae around the lake. We were both pensive and could not find the words to express our thoughts.

I said my goodbyes and retired to my room for a fitful sleep.

Monday morning, I woke and readied myself for the day. Then I escorted Ellie Mae to breakfast for the last time.

After breakfast, I brought the wagon around to her cabin. I loaded the typewriter, her trunk, and her valise in the back. Then I helped her up to the seat before sitting next to her.

As we pulled away, I heard her sniff. When I looked over, she dried her eyes with her handkerchief.

"I'm going to miss them, too," she said. "I adore your mother, father, brothers, and Violet."

"My brothers? Are you sure?" I teased, and she rewarded me with a half-smile.

"Even Boone."

"I promise not to tell him. Wouldn't want his ego to inflate."

We both waved one last time as we crested the hill before the ranch faded out of sight.

I reached into my pocket and gave her my note. "I can't promise this will make you feel better."

She unfolded the paper and read it.

"My love?" she whispered.

"You know you are."

She read it again before folding it up. She reached in the wagon for her satchel and put my words there.

"I'll keep it with your other note."

"My other note?" I did not remember writing her a note before.

"Yes, the one you wrote the first time you used my type-writer."

I laughed. "You kept that? What did I say?"

"You know what you said."

She was right. I remembered.

Too soon we arrived at Lancaster's. I stayed until she received a room. Then we took her typewriter over to the news-paper office. She followed me outside for one last goodbye.

I breathed deeply as I walked to the post office to pick up our mail. Then I climbed into the empty wagon and drove home.

After I finished putting the wagon away and caring for the horses, I entered the ranch house. The sight that greeted me surprised me.

Mama stood. "I'll fix you a plate."

"What's going on?" I asked Papa as I cataloged the men around the table. Next to Papa was Warren Cahill, then Adam Larson, George Larson, and Georgie Larson. Julia sat across from Adam. Mama sat next to Papa.

Georgie spoke first. "After a lot of thinking, I've decided I would like to leave the ranch."

I took a seat between Mama and Julia.

His father, George, added, "I'm in for thirty percent. I'd like you to buy out twenty percent to give to Georgie. That'd leave me and Maggie a ten percent stake to live off."

"Since we split Larson Stables off years ago," Adam said, "I am not looking to inherit any stake in Colter Ranch."

I swallowed hard. A twenty percent buyout was a big deal for the ranch. We'd have to sell some stock to make it happen. I wasn't sure how much without running the numbers.

"What were you thinking about the split between Cahill and Colter?" I asked.

"Colter stake totaling sixty percent. That would be forty for me and twenty for you, Sam," Papa said. "I keep the majority stake. Then thirty for Cahill and ten for George as he has asked."

I rubbed my temples. "I'll need some time to figure out how we'll do it."

"You think you can figure it out by Friday?" Georgie ask-ed. "I'd like to leave for our new place this weekend. Also, I'd prefer to take some stock instead of all cash. That should help us."

"Alright," I said. "Let me see what I can do."

"We'll get the attorneys involved," Papa said. "I'll ride in tomorrow and let them know we want them out here on Wednesday afternoon."

I frowned. "That's when Mama and Ellie Mae leave."

"Say your goodbyes to Ellie Mae when you take your mother into town."

As I pushed away my uneaten sandwich, I thought my plan through. I needed to pore over the books for the ranch. Then come up with a new budget and update the forecast. After calculating the inventory, I would have to adjust the figures. It was overwhelming, especially since we would meet with the attorneys on Wednesday.

They made a few suggestions. I retrieved some paper from my desk and took a few notes.

"We'll need to do a full inventory of the ranch assets," I said. "I'll need some help with a current appraisal of the ranch horses. Adam, Julia, can you handle that?"

They agreed.

"I'll get some men to help with inventory," Warren said.

I did not feel good about it. Not in the slightest. Twenty percent was a fair-sized chunk to buy out. We were off season for a drive to market. We didn't know what the fall calving season would bring. The wild grass was thinner because of the lack of summer rains. Too many things could go wrong.

Handling a buyout was much more problematic than gifting me twenty percent ownership on paper. Adding me was a matter of changing some numbers in the ledger and signing some legal paperwork. Buying out part of the Larson stake meant getting a current valuation of all our assets, cattle, horses, cash on hand, and our joint reserves. I had to find the funds from our personal reserves to cover the jump in ownership from forty-five percent to sixty percent. I hoped we could manage without selling any cattle.

After the Larsons left, I used the dining room table as a workspace. We had one thousand head. If we gave Georgie twenty percent, that would take us down to eight hundred. The new bull and heifers would stay. I would not negotiate that. Those were investments for our future.

Mama graciously served the meal out on the picnic table since it was such a nice day. I worked late into the night.

The next morning, Deacon helped me move all the paperwork out to Ellie Mae's cabin so I could use the table there and Mama could have the dining room table back. I barely took a break for a meal that day.

In the morning, I met with Georgie to clarify a few things. I suggested giving him one-hundred-fifty head. He agreed as long as we threw in a few horses. Also, two of the cowboys wanted to move with him.

Late in the afternoon, I felt like I had a good plan. I found Papa in the barn at his workbench. He looked up as I approached.

"Need some help?" he asked.

I sat on a stool. The smell of hay tickled my nose, and I sneezed several times. When I recovered, I rubbed a hand over my face.

"It's a lot. On the surface, twenty percent doesn't sound like that much. But when I carve it out of our assets, stock, and reserves, it's a fair chunk. I think Warren can cover his extra five percent without issue."

Papa nodded.

I laughed nervously. "Makes me appreciate the generosity of your gift even more."

Papa squeezed my shoulder.

I gave him a few different options for the buyout, and we discussed the merits and drawbacks of each option. We finally agreed on the best way to approach our side of the buyout.

As I turned to leave, he stopped me.

"I'm real proud of you, Sam. I knew if I stayed out of your way, your plan would be solid. It's better than what I was thinking. You've proven, yet again, that you deserve the ownership Hannah and I are giving you."

My heart swelled with pride under his compliment. His trust meant the world to me.

I headed back to Ellie Mae's cabin, aware of how little I thought of her since she left. It made me sad. But I still had to write up everything before we met with the attorneys the next day.

Around midnight, I fell into the bed in the cabin, feeling satisfied that I was prepared.

CHAPTER 22

ELLIE MAE

Tuesday morning, I donned my brown skirt and white shirt. I fixed my hair and gathered my things before heading over to James's office to interview him.

When I arrived at the large brick building, my jaw went slack. I did not know the railroad employed so many office workers. There were at least forty men in the office alone.

The receptionist led me up a flight of stairs and down a long hall to James's office. He motioned me to a seat and told me that Mr. Colter would arrive in a few minutes. I set my things on an empty chair.

A large table stood along one wall. On it sat a large model of the entire railway line from Seligman to Prescott. The model included detailed landmarks of key points along the rail line. A miniature train with six cars sat on the tracks. Along the route stood several signal shacks, as well as each mail drop.

A map of the route was on a wall. On the opposite wall, hung a schematic of the depots in Prescott and Seligman. Several diagrams of the roundhouse depicted how the engine could turn around. To my understanding, they did not build it, which was one of my questions for James.

I glanced at the papers on James's desk. Timetables and other calculations filled most of the papers visible to me without snooping.

"Morning, Ms. Thatcher," James said from the doorway behind me.

"Good morning, Mr. Colter." It seemed odd to use the formal address after having spent the weekend with him at his family's ranch. I was glad he chose the more formal address since I was there in a professional capacity.

I retrieved my notebook and pencil from my satchel. Then I stood in front of the drawings of the roundhouse.

"Is this what it will look like?" I asked.

James stood next to me. He pointed out some key features.

"When does construction begin?"

He led me to a chair. When I sat, he took a seat at his desk.

"We should begin construction on the roundhouse in the next few months."

"No precise date?"

He frowned. I felt a little proud that my persistence frustrated him. That was my job as a journalist. Keep pressing for an answer.

"August is the best time frame I can give at this point."

"Does the construction of the roundhouse fall under your purview?"

"Yes."

"The county granted a bond for building this railroad. The deadline was January first of this year. While the railroad itself goes from Prescott to Seligman and back, wasn't the roundhouse included in the terms of the bond?"

James scowled. He propped his elbows on his desk and leaned forward.

"What are you getting at, Ms. Thatcher?"

"Several sources have stated that it is terribly slow to ride the train from Prescott to Seligman because the train goes in reverse for the entire seventy-six-mile journey. The taxpayers want to know why the roundhouse hasn't been built."

James's lips formed a thin line. "Like I said, construction starts in August."

"Wouldn't the Central Arizona Railway make more money if the train moved faster?"

"Perhaps."

He grew impatient with my questions.

"You will see tomorrow that the experience is not as bad as some of our competitors might have you believe. Would you like a tour of the train station?"

"Surely, we can see that tomorrow morning before we leave. Hannah will want to see it, too."

"Very well."

I asked a few other less controversial questions, which seemed to improve his mood. When I finished with my questions, I asked if I could interview the President, Thomas Bullock.

"Mr. Bullock does not speak to reporters." James's tone was uncompromising.

"I see. Would he be willing to speak with my editor, Clay-ton Williams?"

"Direct your questions to me."

I saw my chance to dig deeper about the inner workings of the railroad.

"Are the rumors true? Bullock and Murphy, the secretary of the railroad, do not get along?"

James stood to his feet and rounded his desk. He moved close to where I sat and leaned against his desk with his leg almost touching mine. He crossed his arms over his chest.

"Come now, Ellie Mae. Let's not be contentious. We still have a long trip ahead of us tomorrow and Thursday."

He flashed a charming smile that did not reach his icy eyes.

I knew he intended to make me uncomfortable. I wanted to angle my legs away from him, but I did not want to give him the satisfaction of seeing me squirm.

"Perhaps we could go to lunch together, so I can tell you more about the inner workings of our railway."

"No, thank you."

He inched closer until his leg touched mine.

I straightened my back. "Does it bother you that Sam and I are sweethearts?"

He narrowed his eyes.

"It does," I said. "You don't understand what I see in him, and it infuriates you."

He stiffened, and I knew my words hit their mark. He moved a few inches away from me.

I softened my approach. "James, I'm not trying to cause friction between you and Sam, or even between you and me. I'm just trying to do my job. The questions I'm asking are ones I've heard whispered by your customers. They like that the railroad is in town, but they also have some concerns."

He looked away from me.

"Wouldn't it be better to answer the questions directly to someone you can trust to represent what you say accurately, rather than let rumors fester?"

His head snapped my direction. "Can I trust you?"

"Of course. You've read my articles. Have I not represent-ed your family fairly?"

James considered my words for a moment. Then he walk-ed over to the door and closed it.

"You did not hear this from me."

I nodded as he sat down at his desk.

"Bullock is being bullish about the second phase of the railway. Part of our commitment to the taxpayers with the bond was to build the railroad from Prescott through Congress and down along the Hassayampa River, then towards Phoenix. Murphy owns the gold mine at Congress, so he has a vested interest in seeing that the line goes through there. Bullock wants to go through the Black Canyon and Bradshaw Mountains. They have been at war over this since they combined their capital last year." James ran a hand through his hair. "Until they come to an agreement, the second phase is on hold. Mining companies in Congress and in the Bradshaw Mountains want the line extended. They each want the line to go near their mines. We can't afford to build both routes."

I jotted some notes down.

"Why are you telling me this?" I asked, as I did not trust his motives.

"If you print something about this 'war', perhaps public opinion could sway them to act."

"I see. Who can corroborate your version of the facts?"

"Frank Murphy. He will be on the train. I'll arrange some time for you to meet with him."

I agreed to hear Frank Murphy out without promising to write what James asked. Something bothered me about his request, but I could not put my finger on it.

After a few more questions, James escorted me downstairs. He asked me to meet him at the train station at ten o'clock for a tour prior to our eleven o'clock departure. I thanked him for his time, then I walked to the newspaper office.

I relayed the more controversial part of our conversation

to my editor.

"I'll bet that Colter is aligning himself with Murphy," Clayton said. "Perhaps Murphy promised him a better position or some other incentive if he gets us to publish something in his favor. I'll ask another reporter to get Bullock's side while you are gone."

After I thanked him, I left to pick up my new dress from the dressmaker. The dress was for the train ride. I hoped it would make me look like a professional reporter instead of a farmer's daughter.

When I carried my new dress home to my room at Lancaster's, I wondered what Sam might think of the new dress. It differed from my plain farm dresses. I hoped he liked it.

The rest of the evening, I went over my notes and added additional details that came to mind as I reflected on my inter-view with James. Then I retired for the evening, full of anticipation for my first train ride.

CHAPTER 23

SAM

On Wednesday morning, immediately following breakfast, I hitched up the wagon to take Mama into town for her
train ride. She wore her Sunday dress of sapphire blue with
black lace and her matching hat. The dress made her look
younger than her age of forty-five. Her eyes lit with excitement as I climbed up in the wagon seat next to her.

"I'm so glad you convinced me to take this trip. You
wanted me to watch out for Ellie Mae's welfare, but I am
also looking forward to seeing what James does."

"Thank you, Mama."

"Plus, I'll be the first Colter besides James to ride on a
train. I'm sure Deacon and Preston will ply me for every detail when I return."

"Boone might be pretty interested as well," I said absent-
mindedly.

"What's wrong, Sam?"

I sighed heavily. "This buyout. I know Papa and I
agreed on a plan. I'm just nervous about depleting our reserves so much. One little unexpected problem could really
hurt us."

She patted my arm. "You were wrapped up in figuring it

out on your own, but remember to trust the Lord. Pray about it too."

Mama was right. I had forgotten to pray. I just plowed ahead, trying to work it all out on my own. Before my head hit the pillow that night, I would pray.

We arrived at the train station around nine-thirty. James waited in the stationmaster's office, so I escorted Mama there. Since I had other things to do, I promised to be back before eleven.

I checked in at the butcher shop. Then I stopped by the post office. I flipped through the letters, and one stood out to me. It had a Chino Valley return address.

My hands shook as I tore it open.

Dear Mr. Colter,

Thank you for your honest words. I will grant you my permission to court Ellie Mae. However, prior to an engagement, I require that you meet with me. My family and I will be at the Independence Day celebration in a few weeks. We will stay overnight at Lancaster's, so you should plan to speak with me that evening without Ellie Mae.

Regards,

Lee Thatcher

I reread the letter. My excitement grew until my eyes snagged on the word "however." I supposed his request made sense, given that I was a stranger to him. It still left me feeling unsettled, especially since Ellie Mae and I had grown so close already. If Mr. Thatcher deemed me as an unacceptable match for his daughter, it would break both our hearts.

I folded the letter and stuffed it back into the envelope. I placed it, along with the other mail, in my satchel. Between the buyout and the less than enthusiastic response from Ellie Mae's father, I arrived at the train station with a passel of anxiety.

I found Mama with James. He took her on a tour of the inner workings of the station. A woman in a very modern rust and black dress stood with them. When Mama spotted me, the woman turned around. I could hardly believe my eyes. It was Ellie Mae, and she looked stunning in her new dress.

The air left my lungs as they approached me. The dress emphasized Ellie Mae's curves, tempting me to haul her off to the courthouse and marry her on the spot.

"Sam," she greeted me. Her eyes shone with deep affection. Then she frowned. "You look exhausted."

I pulled her away from Mama and James. When I faced her, I rested my hands on her hips. She placed her hands behind my neck. She looked heavenly.

"What's wrong?" she asked.

"Mama can fill you in on the details. The short version of the story is that Georgie Larson wants us to buyout his stake in the ranch and I have been working late for the past few days trying to figure out how to make it happen."

She placed a hand on my cheek.

"I've missed you," she said.

I studied her eyes. Then my gaze dropped to her lips. I looked away, lest I kiss her senseless in front of my mama.

"I received a letter from your father."

"Oh? What did he say?"

"We may court, but he wants to meet me on the fourth. Your family is coming to town for the big celebration."

She pulled me into a hug. "That's wonderful news!"

When she leaned back, I held her closer. Then I lowered

my lips to hers. I searched and teased with some restraint. I tried to find the balance between expressing my love for her in that kiss and not embarrassing her in front of my family. When she returned my kiss fervently, I struggled not to kiss her more deeply.

My heart raced faster than a train. I let my hands move over her back as her hands explored mine. I loved her and could barely contain myself.

When Mama coughed loudly, I slowed and then ended the kiss. Ellie Mae pulled away. Her cheeks were rosy and her lips red and plump from the kiss. Had we been alone, I was certain I would have kissed her again.

"I love you," I whispered in ragged breaths.

"I love you, Sam."

A train whistle blew, and she jumped back. Her smile reinforced her words from a moment ago. She loved me, Sam, the young man trying to figure out his place in the Colter family. My heart soared.

"We need to board the train," James said as he touched Ellie Mae's arm.

"I'll see you on Thursday afternoon?" I asked.

She nodded.

Then James whisked her and Mama away. They found a seat in the first car and Ellie Mae waved to me. I waved as the train backed out of the station.

Lord, keep them safe.

I headed for the wagon. My heart filled with love for my woman as I rode home.

My joy was short-lived. Once I arrived at the ranch, the Larsons, Warren Cahill, our attorneys, and Papa waited for me at the ranch house. They must have been waiting awhile because Preston volunteered to care for the horses and put the wagon away. I retrieved my satchel and hurried into the house.

CHAPTER 24

ELLIE MAE

As Hannah and I boarded the train and James led us to our seats, the flush from Sam's kiss lingered on my cheeks. I sat near the window so I could wave to Sam. My pulse fluttered as a smile spread across his face when he waved in return.

"We are courting now," I whispered.

Hannah must have heard me. "He received word from your father, then?"

I turned to look at her. "Yes. Papa is going to bring the family down for the fourth of July festivities."

"How wonderful! I look forward to meeting them."

The train started in motion. All the seats on the train faced toward the engine, but the motion of the train moved backwards. It took several miles to get used to the unnatural motion of backing the train down the tracks.

I faced the back of the train. The excitement I expected to see on the passengers' faces never appeared. Many wore looks of confusion or annoyance. The backwards motion caused anxiety in one woman in particular. There was an empty seat next to her, so I sat down.

"Morning. My name is Ms. Thatcher. What's yours?" I

asked her.

She was a middle-aged woman of some girth. She wore a stylish bustle dress in a dark green. Her fingers gripped the edge of the armrests.

"Mrs. Beale."

"A pleasure to meet you. Is this your first ride on the train?"

She nodded vehemently.

"Mine, too."

"It is unnerving to travel backwards," she said in a shaky voice.

"Take a deep breath. Good. Now let it out."

She gave me a half smile.

"I'm sure we'll get used to it soon."

"Thank you."

"May I ask what brings you on the train today?"

She relaxed in her seat as she told me. She lived in Prescott with her husband. He rode up on the train yesterday for some business in Flagstaff. He was due to meet her back in Selig-man that evening. They would travel back to Prescott in the morning together.

"He told me it would be fun to ride the train. I'm still waiting for the fun part."

I smiled. "Well, you've made one new friend already. I live in Prescott too. Perhaps we can meet for lunch one day soon?"

Her face lit with excitement. "I would like that."

"Ms. Thatcher," James said my name. I looked up.

"Mr. Murphy would like to speak with you."

"Of course. It was nice to meet you, Mrs. Beale."

I followed James to the last car on the very short train. Besides the engine, a freight and baggage car, there were only three passenger cars. A large vestibule adjoined the last car. Mr. Murphy stood in the vestibule, smoking a pipe.

James introduced me before he went back inside the car. He stood near the door, presumably to keep anyone from interrupting my conversation with Mr. Murphy.

"Good morning, Ms. Thatcher. James tells me you are a re-porter with the Gazette?"

"Yes. He mentioned you wanted to speak with me."

He motioned his hand toward the vista. "Isn't this love-ly?"

I admired the view. The train moved so slowly it changed little. To my right, we passed a large rock for-mation that jut-ted out of the ground like a large hand with distinct round fingers.

"Before construction began, there were two competing bids for a line from Prescott to Seligman. Thomas Bullock was one entrepreneur. My brother N. O. Murphy was the other. The A&P, that is the Atlantic & Pacific, approached both men. They negotiated a merger between my brother's company and Bullock's. One major condition to that agreement was that the line from Prescott to Phoenix would go past Congress and my mining interests there. Bullock agreed, as I later learned, to just about anything in order to have his name associated with this railway."

Mr. Murphy puffed on his pipe then blew out the smoke.

"The A&P does not care about the animosity and in-fighting in our railway. They want freight shipped from Prescott and the area ranches up to Seligman. The A&P al-ways wanted a line out of Prescott but did not want to man-age it. They are focused on linking the west to the east. They throw their support and some resources behind a feeder line, like ours, but they don't want to manage the feeder lines."

"So, why is there so much infighting?" I asked.

"Bullock. Or as we fondly call him, Bully-lock. He signed papers agreeing to build the line from Prescott to Phoenix through Congress. Except now he is trying to change the route completely. He pulled a coup earlier this year to get my brother and most of his supporters voted off the board. I'm the only one left in the company, besides James, who fights for the Congress route."

"Why are you telling me this? Your plan for the route serves your own selfish motives."

Mr. Murphy narrowed his eyes as he puffed on his pipe.

"They defined the route in a legal and binding document. You are correct, that it is in my best interest to have the line go by my copper mine. The proposal benefits my employees, their families, as well as my interests. They could travel to see family. They would receive the newest inventions and materials from the east. My primary motivation is to see the legal obligation fulfilled."

"Why not go to court?"

He sighed. He seemed frustrated with my lack of business knowledge. I was having a hard time connecting my potential articles with his desired outcome.

"A legal battle would bankrupt the line and possibly lead to its demise. That would cause a breach of contract with the A&P. A battle in the press costs significantly less. Yes, it requires I divulge some of the internal conflict within the company, but it also puts pressure on Bullock to fulfill his agreement."

"Won't he just fire you and James?"

"He can't."

I frowned. Mr. Murphy's glare warned me not to ask more questions. He gave a sharp nod to James. James stepped out into the vestibule.

"Ms. Thatcher, you have your confirmation of the story. Now do your part to see that it ends up in print."

Mr. Murphy turned away from me. James escorted me back into the car. I did not like Mr. Murphy's tone. James's next words did little to ease my concerns.

"You need to run that article, Ellie Mae. I can't protect you from Murphy and his men."

I took my seat next to Hannah for the rest of the trip. When we arrived in Seligman several hours later, I asked many random passengers about their impressions of the trip. I took down their names and their reactions to use in my articles.

Then James showed us around the Seligman station. I added to my notes from the morning. He checked us into our hotel. Both Hannah and I freshened up before meeting him in the hotel dining room for supper.

Hannah carried the conversation. She plied James with dozens of questions about his job. I paid attention for a while, except my mind kept going back to Mr. Murphy's words. It was a threat. I didn't like being threatened. Yet, I also had no way of defending myself against an unknown threat. Unless Clayton told me otherwise, I would write the article about the turmoil inside the Central Arizona Railway. It was news-worthy information.

We retired to our rooms. I got very little sleep between the gunshots further down the main street in town and the loud music coming from a nearby saloon. Seemed Seligman was the stereotypical wild western town.

The next morning, I readied myself and donned my rust dress again. It made no sense to bring a second dress for another day of travel. When I met Hannah in the lobby, it seemed she felt the same way as she wore her sapphire blue dress again.

James took us to the station. The train departed at ten.

The forward motion of the train was a vast improvement. The engine moved noticeably faster than the day before. I found Mrs. Beale and her husband. She agreed with my opinion of the forward motion.

An hour into the trip, a monsoon storm broke loose. Thun-der rippled overhead. Lightning shot to the ground. I stood to look out the window as we entered Big Chino Wash.

Then I saw it.

A wall of muddy water rushed toward the train. It hit our car hard. Glass windows shattered. I flew through the air until my back hit the roof of the car hard. Air whooshed from my lungs. Gravity pulled me down. My ribs connected with the side of a seat. Pain tore through my side as I tried to breathe.

The light in the car dimmed. I tried to crawl forward, disoriented. I moved up and over one seat. Then the next. The car was on its side. The car pushed away from the track as another surge hit it.

"Hannah!" I called out.

Rain poured through the shattered windows above me. Water rose to my ankles, then my knees as I tried to push forward despite the added weight of my drenched skirts.

"James! Hannah!" I cried out for Sam's family in the dark car.

"Ellie Mae!" Hannah's voice met my ears.

I found her. Her leg wedged underneath the seat. Water rose to her waist.

"James! Your mother needs your help!"

Another minute passed as the water inched up to her bust line. I threw my hat off. Then I took a deep breath and plunged my head under the murky water. I felt around for her foot and dislodged it. When I came up, I helped her stand on the edge of the seat.

"Where is James?" Hannah asked.

When I searched for him, I could not find him.

I made sure Hannah was fine. Thankfully, the water stopped rising and receded out the open windows at the bottom of the tilted car.

I pushed forward to the door at the front of the car. It would not budge open. Several men came, tried to open it, and failed.

"Boost me up to the window," I asked one rather burly man.

He did.

My lithe frame shimmied through the opening. It would not be an option for many of the passengers.

The rain pelted my hair and ran in streams down my neck and shoulders, soaking my entire dress.

I crawled along the top of the car. "We need help!"

I shaded my eyes with my hand. The car behind ours suffered a similar fate. The last two cars remained upright. Several men exited the upright cars and made their way toward the two overturned cars.

When the car shifted again, I grabbed onto the frame of a shattered window. I ignored the pain as broken glass shredded my palm.

A man wearing a railroad uniform crawled toward me.

"Are you alright?" he yelled over the loud hiss of the pouring rain.

"Yes. The doors won't open. I squeezed through the window, but others won't be able to."

He crawled to the window that I had escaped from. "You crawled through that?"

I nodded. He looked me over as if he found the idea unlikely.

He leaned over the opening and asked the passengers to clear the area below. Then he stood and stomped on the window frame with his foot until it collapsed inside the car. The opening without the window frame was much larger. He leaned over the edge and helped the women and children up as other passengers boosted them from below.

"My baby!" I heard one woman screaming frantically as she emerged from the window.

"It's alright," I reassured her. "We will find your baby." I pointed her towards the back of the train. "Crawl along the cars. The men at the end will help you up the bank."

Hannah was one of the last women to emerge from the window. She carried a small bundle close to her chest. Tears blurred her eyes. "He didn't make it. But I will take him to his mama, anyway. She'll need to see him to believe he is gone."

Tears trickled down my face, intermingled with the rain.

A man barked orders nearby. His voice sounded familiar. Then I saw him. James stood atop the baggage car, exclaiming to the engineer and several other railroad employees.

I was going to head toward James, but a man appeared to escort me along the cars to the back of the train. I jumped from our car to the next just before it shifted again.

I found Hannah on the bank. She tended to the injured.

"Do you have anything in there?" she pointed at my satchel still slung across my body. I didn't remember even putting it on.

"Just paper and pencils. I saw James. He's alright."

She nodded. "Can you spare some of your petticoat?"

I tore off several strips and handed them to her.

Despite the continued onslaught of rain, I looked

around. Passengers lined the bank. Most were in shock. Several had gashes on their faces, arms, or hands. The woman with the baby cradled the dead child and sobbed.

A loud creaking sound came from the overturned cars. The large man that I met on top of the car looked my direction. He stood and ran toward us as the car upended. His body dis-appeared under the car and a wall of mud and water.

I looked away. At least two people did not survive. I saw James on the other bank. His face looked grim.

Hannah continued to look over each passenger on the shore. Many sat huddled together. No one else emerged from the cars. Only those on the banks survived.

Finally, Hannah came to sit next to me.

"Your hands. Let me see them."

I turned them over and exposed my palms.

She picked out the shards of broken glass. The rain washed away my blood as soon as it hit the surface of my skin. After several minutes, she wrapped a strip of petticoat around them.

In the rain, we huddled together and prayed for the passengers and the railroad management. We prayed for the rain to stop and for everyone's safety.

CHAPTER 25

SAM

Thursday morning dawned in a gloomy sky. All signs pointed to a long day of monsoon storms. It would be a miser-able wagon ride to town to pick up Mama and Ellie Mae from the train. Preston drew the short straw for that duty. I stuffed down my disappointment. I wanted to be there when Ellie Mae arrived.

Instead, I led the trip to the stockyards to sell fifty head. It had to be done to meet the terms of the buyout agreement. If the stockyards refused to take them, then I would sell the rest at Fort Whipple.

I saddled up Bailey and donned a slicker, as rain already misted the air. Deacon and two cowboys rounded up the fifty head, and we drove them over the mountain toward the stockyards. The trip seemed longer than normal as the rain grew steadily more forceful. I kept my hat low to keep the rain off my face.

As if going to the stockyards was not enough, we drove cattle through the pounding rain. I'll admit I did not have fond thoughts of Georgie Larson at that moment.

When we arrived at the stockyards, they only took twenty-five head. Until the rain cleared, they could not accommodate more.

We drove the rest of the cattle to Fort Whipple. It took me thirty minutes to negotiate with the supply officer before he finally agreed to take the twenty-five head. He extracted a promise from me that Eddie would help slaughter some of them next week. Eddie would help us out, even if he wouldn't be happy about it.

I swung by the train station on the way back through town. There was no word about the train's arrival. The stationmaster said it should have arrived by then despite the rain. I found Preston, and he confirmed the stationmaster told him the same. He agreed to stay and wait as long as it took.

I headed home.

After I took care of Bailey, Papa found me in the barn. Deep lines etched near his worried eyes.

"Any word from your mother?"

I shook my head. "Stationmaster thinks there's been a delay because of the rain."

We walked back to the house where I laid my slicker across one of the rocking chairs on the porch. Then I scraped the mud from my boots and left them outside to dry so as not to mar Mama's clean floors.

Penny greeted me and offered me a sandwich. I took it and ate as I climbed the stairs to my room. I finished the sandwich and changed out of my wet clothes.

The rain finally stopped at supper time. We delayed the meal, waiting for Preston, Mama, and Ellie Mae, though I was not sure Ellie Mae would come to the ranch. I hoped so.

Preston returned with an empty wagon around seven.

Papa paced back and forth. As worried as I was, I could have paced too. But I stayed seated at the table.

As soon as Preston opened the door, Papa asked, "Where

is she?"

"The stationmaster got a telegram that the Seligman station lost contact with them around ten-thirty this morning."

"Lost contact?"

"That's all he said."

Penny set out the over-cooked supper. None of us minded. We were worried about Mama, and I was worried about Ellie Mae. I helped Penny with the dishes, eager to do something. Then I joined my papa and brothers in the parlor.

Boone was out in the wilderness on an extended surveying trip. Deacon, Preston, and I discussed what we could do after Papa sent Violet to bed.

"We should ride out along the tracks to find them," I suggested.

"They could be anywhere," Papa said. "Some of those areas aren't accessible by wagon."

"What if we rode up to Chino Valley and then towards Seligman?" Deacon suggested.

"We need more information," Preston said. "It's a fool's errand to take off without knowing where they are."

"James would send word," Papa said.

I was not too sure about that. If something bad happened, his position with the railroad would take priority over family loyalty.

"We need to do something," I said.

Papa stood. "Let's pray then get some shuteye. We'll head to town in the morning."

So, that's what we did. We gathered and prayed for Mama, Ellie Mae, and James.

Every time I woke throughout the night, I prayed until I fell back asleep.

The next morning, we left Warren Cahill in charge.

Penny watched Violet. The four of us saddled up our horses and headed into town. The stationmaster provided an update.

"Tracks got washed out at Big Chino Wash," he said to the sizeable crowd gathered at the station.

"That's only an hour outside of Seligman," someone from the crowd said.

"The railway has hired stagecoaches to bring the passengers back to town. If you have the means to retrieve your loved ones, then we suggest you see to it."

Papa frowned. His jaw twitched. "I never should have agreed to this."

I agreed, but said nothing.

We didn't discuss a thing. We just pointed our horses north out of town toward Chino Valley. Once we were in Chino Valley, we stopped for some food. We purchased some meat and cheese for ourselves and for Mama and Ellie Mae. Then we placed it in our saddlebags and headed toward Big Chino Wash, still several hours away.

Each time I worried, I prayed. I prayed that Mama and Ellie Mae were safe. Hopefully, we would find them quickly. I prayed for James despite the tension that had entered our relationship weeks ago. He was still my brother. I wanted him returned safely too.

It was mid-afternoon by the time we arrived on the banks of Big Chino Wash.

Then we saw it.

Mud mired the engine. It was some distance from what remained of the train tracks. Further downstream, an overturned passenger car's wheels and underbelly glinted in the sunlight. The car behind it laid on its side. Two more cars, also off the tracks, tilted at odd angles stuck in the drying mud.

The water in the wash was stagnant and shallow. How much water did it take to overturn a railroad car?

My stomach clenched at the sight. My eyes scanned the area. There was no one near the train. Then I searched along the opposite bank. A group of people stood huddled around several small fires.

I looked for Mama's sapphire dress and Ellie Mae's rust dress. I could not see them.

Papa kicked his horse into a trot down the bank and through the wash. The rest of us followed behind.

"Let's split up," Deacon suggested. He kicked his horse toward the far end of the camp. Preston followed.

Papa and I searched the faces of each woman. We asked if anyone had seen Mama or Ellie Mae.

"Ms. Thatcher was so kind to me," a plump woman said.

I held my breath as hope started to rise.

"She sat with me when the train first started toward Selig-man yesterday. I haven't seen her since."

My gut fell to my knees.

We met Deacon and Preston in the middle.

"A few folks mentioned a woman helped bandage cuts and scrapes," Preston said.

"That sounds like Hannah," Papa said.

"But they haven't seen her since yesterday afternoon."

Deep lines crossed Papa's forehead as he frowned.

"No word about Ellie Mae or James?"

Deacon shook his head.

My heart squeezed so tightly I thought I might keel over. I dismounted my horse.

"Do you have water?" a woman asked. She had two young children. "We've had nothing to drink all day."

I handed her my canteen. "Ration it out."

She nodded. As I walked away, I heard her say, "All our

angels have such brilliant blue eyes."

I turned back. "What did you mean by that?"

"The woman who helped us yesterday had the same eyes as you."

"Have you seen her? Or a woman with sandy brown hair in a rust-colored dress?"

"Not since yesterday."

I joined Papa and my brothers at the far end of the camp. The sun was low in the sky, so we built a fire. We shared what water and food we had with the women and children, wondering where Mama and Ellie Mae could be.

CHAPTER 26

ELLIE MAE

The rain finally stopped in the late afternoon the day of the accident. Hannah and I helped as many people as possible. As we walked toward the tracks, we spotted James and men from the railroad. They stood beside a hand-powered railcar.

"James," Hannah said. "You must do something for these people. How far are we from Seligman?"

James shifted uncomfortably as Mr. Murphy joined us.

"Mama, we're handling it."

"Nonsense. These people are hungry and thirsty," Hannah said.

"Mrs. Colter?" Mr. Murphy asked. She nodded. "Why don't you and your friend ride back to Seligman with us? You can personally oversee the loading of provisions."

Hannah nodded. James helped her onto the manual railcar. Then he helped me. The four of us and the railcar operator barely fit on it.

Hours later, at dusk, we arrived in Seligman. Mr. Murphy escorted us to the mercantile. He promised to pay the owner for whatever food and provisions we purchased. Then he went to the train station to buy a wagon and horses.

After we loaded a wagon full of supplies, we stayed in town. It was too late in the day to venture back out. Mr. Murphy reserved a hotel room for us. James was nowhere to be seen, so Mr. Murphy escorted us to supper.

"Where is James?" Hannah asked.

"He is coordinating the rescue efforts and asking for all available stagecoaches and wagons to rendezvous in Seligman as early in the morning as possible. He's arranging for some engineers to survey the damage. They will figure out how to get the train moving again."

I could not help but ask the obvious question. "Why isn't there a bridge over the wash? It seems dangerous to build a railroad in the bottom of a wash, knowing monsoons could do exactly what this one did."

Mr. Murphy frowned at me. "The construction team felt it was an acceptable risk. We so rarely have such strong monsoon storms."

"Yet, we did today. At least two people lost their lives. Possibly more."

Mr. Murphy looked down at his food. "That loss grieves us at the Central Arizona Railway. We are doing all we can to care for the passengers."

Tension covered the rest of the meal. Hannah and I retired to our rooms. I didn't bother trying to clean my dress. I doubted it would dry by the morning.

The next morning, a man in a Central Arizona Railway uniform led us to the loaded wagon. We headed out along a circuitous route to Big Chino Wash. It was late afternoon by the time we found the camp.

"Ellie Mae!"

When I heard my name called, I turned to see Sam as the wagon stopped. I jumped down from the wagon and ran to him.

He hugged me close and kissed my face and my lips. "Thank God. You are alright."

I looked up at him, not releasing my hold. "What are you doing here?"

"Rescuing you, but it looks like you are busy." He winked at me.

"Your mother is incredible. She bullied our way onto the railcar with James. Then she got Mr. Murphy to pay for all these supplies. It's going to be several days before they can transport everyone out."

"Papa!" Sam called out as he released me.

Will ran toward his wife and swept her up in his arms. He kissed her like he hadn't seen her in a year. I was a little jealous until I reminded myself that Sam and I were only courting.

"Tell me your plan," Will said to his wife as Deacon and Preston joined us.

"We have water for everyone. Let's stoke up these fires so we can feed these folks. Use crates for the fire if need be," Hannah said.

Several women helped warm up food. Sam and I handed out bread to every person in the camp. We had several loaves leftover, which would keep for the next day.

Deacon and Preston handed out the tin bowls and mugs that we purchased from the mercantile. Then the passengers lined up for beans and stew. Sam and I waited at the end of the line.

Hannah was strong in a crisis. I wondered if the wagon train west honed her instinct. She took charge unlike Mr. Murphy or James or any of the railroad employees. Everyone had food, water, and medical care because of her. She knew exactly what to do.

"You should be proud of your mama," I said to Sam as we sat down on the ground near the fire the Colter boys built.

"I am. I'm proud of you, too. You probably have a story half written already."

After we finished eating, he took my hand and rubbed his thumb over my knuckles.

I smiled and tapped my temple. "Up here. My paper disintegrated when it got wet yesterday. Some of my notes are still legible. But I won't be writing anything until I get back to town."

I yawned as the stress of the last day washed over me.

"You should lie down. Get some rest," Sam said.

Will placed his saddle on my left and Sam's saddle on my right. Then he stared Sam down. "Only one doing any cuddling with his woman tonight is me."

"Yes, sir," Sam said as his face turned red. "Good night, Ellie Mae."

"Good night, Sam."

As I laid down on the ground, I turned my back to him so I wouldn't be tempted to gawk at him in the firelight.

The next morning, I woke. Both saddles were gone. So were Will and Sam.

"I sent them to Garland Ranch to see if the owner can help bring folks to Chino Valley or Prescott," Hannah said. "They should be back this afternoon."

Throughout the afternoon, wagons and stagecoaches arrived to take passengers either to Chino Valley or Prescott. By the time Will and Sam returned, only half the passengers remained.

The Garland Ranch men drove a wagonload of folks down to Chino Valley. They made two trips, leaving only a dozen passengers, the Colters, and myself.

"Sam, can you take me to Prescott? Is there enough day-light left?" I asked him.

"Why the urgency?" he asked.

"I have articles to write. Because I lived through it, I have the most accurate details about the train derailment and res-cue efforts."

"Take Preston with you," Will said.

Sam mounted his horse, and Preston gave me a leg up to sit behind Sam. I placed my arms loosely around his waist.

"I could get used to this," Sam whispered as he started his horse at a walk.

"Me too."

I wanted to hold on tighter, but with his younger broth-er along for the ride, I knew I had no legitimate reason to. We saw the lights of the town as the sun dipped below the horizon. Sam pulled to a stop in front of the newspaper of-fice at half-past seven.

He dismounted and then helped me down.

"Would you like to freshen up or eat some food?" he ask-ed.

"I'd love to, but if I hope to get the first article ready for the morning edition, I must start writing now."

He leaned down and kissed me briefly. Enough to make me miss him before he was gone.

"Thank you for coming to find us. See you soon?" I asked.

"Probably not until Friday, unless you plan to come out to the ranch."

I shook my head. Then I entered the newspaper office.

Since it was Sunday night, I expected the office to be va-cant. Instead, there was a full crew.

"Ellie Mae!" Clayton called my name. "You look worse for wear."

"I'm fine."

"We heard the reports as some passengers arrived back this afternoon. What can you tell us?"

All the reporters stopped working and gave me their full attention. I recounted the story with as much detail and accuracy as I could. When I finished, Clayton suggested I head home and come back after I cleaned up.

"Alright, but the story about Mrs. Colter is mine to write."

He agreed.

It was well after eight o'clock by the time I arrived at the boardinghouse. Millie agreed to draw me a bath in her private room. She headed over to my room to retrieve a clean dress and undergarments while she waited for the water to heat.

"What color was this dress?" she asked.

"Rust. It was brand new, too."

"Such a shame. I can try to launder it for you tomorrow."

I looked down at the holes in the silk fabric. Dried dirt coated the length of the dress.

"It's destined for the rubbish bin," I said. "Thanks for the offer, though."

Millie dumped the last pail of warm water into the bath and left. It took me longer than I expected, especially since so much dirt was stuck in my hair. By the time I finished, the water was a nasty dark brown. At least I was clean.

After I dressed, I dried my hair with a towel and then Millie braided it for me. I returned to the newspaper office.

The place buzzed with activity. Clayton and a senior reporter read draft articles and sent them back to reporters for corrections. A few reporters asked me some clarifying quest-ions. When everyone had the answers they needed, I sat down at my typewriter.

Then I wrote the story. "Rancher's Wife Saves the Day." Within twenty minutes, I finished typing the article and gave it to Clayton to read.

He looked up at me after he marked corrections for me. "You gonna marry her son?"

"Sam?"

"He's the one who kissed you out front, right?"

My face warmed. "I suppose we'll have to wait and see when he asks."

"You should add 'dream mother-in-law' to the list of your descriptions." He winked to let me know he was not serious.

I sat down and retyped the article with Clayton's sugges-ions. He scanned it then sent it over to the typesetter.

Papers rolled off the printing press. He handed me the first edition. "For posterity's sake. You are the reason this edition is great. Thank you for everything."

"Thank you," I said as I looked down at my story's head-line sprawled across the front page. "Can you send a few to Colter Ranch?"

"Sure thing."

"And one to James Colter and Frank Murphy. I'm sure they won't be pleased, but they should take it as an oppor-tunity to learn from their mistakes."

Clayton laughed. "I think you are tougher than Hannah Colter. Go home and get some rest. Take tomorrow off. We'll see you on Tuesday."

It was four o'clock in the morning by the time I fell into bed. I was a part of the biggest story the town had seen since the capital moved back in 1878 and it felt great.

CHAPTER 27

SAM

I woke the next morning to the sound of Mama cooking breakfast in the kitchen. Since they took a more direct route home, Mama, Papa, and Deacon arrived at the ranch before we did.

The sound of rapid hoofbeats coming down the lane caught my attention. A young man skidded his horse to a stop. He tossed a few copies of a newspaper on the porch before I could reach him. The rider turned his horse back up the lane and rode out of sight.

I reached down and picked up the bundle of newspapers.

"Rancher's Wife Saves the Day by E. M. Thatcher," I read aloud as I entered the house. I set the other copies on the table.

Boone arrived back from his trip while we were gone. He took one paper and read it aloud.

"Mrs. William Colter of Colter Ranch, along with this reporter, were passengers on the Central Arizona Railway on Thursday morning. The train left Seligman around ten o'clock and encountered a heavy monsoon storm shortly afterward."

Preston picked up the narrative. "The passengers describe-ed Mrs. Colter's efforts as that of a brilliant blue-eyed angel. As passengers helped each other to safety, Mrs. Colter quickly took care of their medical needs. She bandaged up the wound-ed."

Deacon continued. "She left the scene to go with representatives of the company into Seligman, where she organized provisions for the stranded passengers. This reporter traveled along with Mrs. Colter back to the camp along the banks of Big Chino Wash the next day. Mrs. Colter single-handedly organized the women at the camp to make meals for the large group of passengers."

"Mama, you're a hero," Violet said.

Mama smiled.

Preston continued reading the article. "She tells how you organized some men to head to Garland's ranch to assist with the rescue efforts."

I smiled as I reread the story. Ellie Mae took none of the credit, even though she helped Mama.

"I can't believe she wrote an entire article about me," Mama said after Papa blessed breakfast.

"I wouldn't be here if it wasn't for her. My foot was caught, and the water rose in the car all the way up to here." Mama pointed to just below her neck. "She freed my foot and helped me get to safety."

Mama told us all how Ellie Mae helped her as she organized things. "I could not have done it without her."

Then Mama looked directly at me. "You better marry that woman. Once word gets out about her contribution to the rescue and that she's a single woman, you'll have some competition."

My face warmed. I thought about Ellie Mae's letter to me on my birthday. I wasn't worried. She had eyes only for me.

174

Preston scoffed. "Not likely. Ellie Mae thinks Sam is the only man to walk the face of the earth."

I smiled from ear to ear. That was my woman.

After breakfast, I met with Warren for an update on the buyout. Georgie and his family moved out of their house. They took only what we agreed to in the buyout settlement. Aunt Julia's family moved into Georgie's old house. All was well at the ranch.

So, I rode into Prescott to spend some time with Ellie Mae. I dismounted Bailey outside of the newspaper office, but her editor told me he gave her the day off. I walked across the street to Lancaster's and Paul took my horse for me. Millie fetched Ellie Mae from her room.

"Morning, beautiful," I said when she met me on the porch. "I see you look refreshed. No more clumps of dirt in your hair."

"You don't look so bad yourself," she teased back. "It surprised me when Millie said you were here."

"We read your article this morning and I had to come see you. Mama told us you saved her life. Thank you."

"It was nothing."

It was significant to us.

"Care for some lunch?" I asked as I offered her my arm.

"I would love some."

She took my arm, and we walked to Isabel's. I smiled when the server seated us in front of the windows. That seem-ed to be our spot. We ordered. I sipped some iced tea while we waited for our food to arrive.

My heart wanted to say a dozen things to her, but my mouth seemed inarticulate in that moment.

"I only just woke up before you arrived," she said. "I did not make it home until four."

"I'm glad Clayton gave you the day off. After I head

home, take it easy."

"This last week has been a whirlwind. You mentioned Papa gave his permission for a courtship. Did he say anything else?"

My smile faded as I recalled the words of his letter. "He in-sists on meeting me before he would consent to anything more."

"I see."

The server set our food on the table.

I continued, "I suppose that makes sense. If it was my daughter, I would not consent to a courtship without meeting the fellow."

She looked away and frowned. "I told him how much I care for you. It hurts a little that he doesn't trust my judgement."

I reached for her hand. "Do not be mad at him. He just wants to protect you."

She changed the subject. "I think James is in trouble."

Then she told me about her interview with James and how he tried to intimidate her and the subsequent conversation with Mr. Murphy.

"They want me to write an article about some internal conflict. James said to me he could not 'protect me from Murphy's men.' I don't know what that means."

My jaw tightened. If James was involved in something that brought harm to Ellie Mae, he would answer to me.

"Have you told Clayton?"

"No. I'll talk to him tomorrow. I'll write an article that will pacify Mr. Murphy. They think they can threaten me to get me to write something they want. I would only write it because it is newsworthy."

"Please be careful," I said.

"I will."

When we finished our meal, I walked Ellie Mae back to the boardinghouse and promised to see her next week.

CHAPTER 28

Prescott, Arizona Territory
July 4, 1887

ELLIE MAE

I saw very little of Sam for the two weeks following the train accident. I was busy writing multiple articles about the accident and the Central Arizona Railway. So, when the fourth of July arrived, I eagerly dressed for my day. I wore a new yellow dress that I purchased the previous week to replace the one that was damaged in the train accident.

When Sam arrived, I smiled at his outfit. He wore a light gray baseball uniform with dark blue letters across his chest that said: "Colter Cowboys."

"I've missed you," he said.

I stood on my tiptoes and kissed his cheek. "Me, too."

He offered me his arm.

"You have uniforms?" I laughed as I took his arm.

"Yup. Papa bought them two years ago. He wanted our name everywhere if we were going to have our own team."

"What's the other team?"

"Prescott Merchants."

He led me to the stands at the baseball field. I sat next to

Violet. Hannah sat between her and Will.

Sam looked serious as he warmed up. He threw the ball to each of his brothers and the cowboys out on the field. His pitches flew from his hand so quickly I barely saw where they landed. He looked in better form than when I watched him practice several weeks ago at the ranch.

During the game, every time Sam caused an out, I cheered loudly. I screamed like a crazy woman when one of the Merchants hit the ball and Boone caught it, then threw it to Sam. Sam threw it to home plate and Preston tagged the runner out just before he started his slide home.

The game flew by. The Merchants fought valiantly. In the end, the Colter Cowboys walked away with a win by two points.

As the crowd thinned, I caught sight of familiar faces as they made their way toward me.

"Papa!" I ran toward my family and gave Papa a hug. In that moment, time melted away as Papa hugged me back.

"It's so good to see you," he said as his voice caught.

"Mama!" I hugged her.

"Ellie Mae, look at you. You look like a full-grown woman in that beautiful dress."

Then I nodded to my younger brother, Grady. I knew he would not appreciate a hug.

"Hey sis," he greeted me. His tone sounded nonchalant, but he gave me a smile. I thought he missed me, too.

Sam joined us. He shifted from foot to foot as he stood next to me.

"Papa, Mama, Grady, this is Sam Colter. Sam, this is my papa, Lee Thatcher, my mama, Amy, and my little brother, who is not so little anymore, Grady."

"Pleased to meet you." Sam wiped his hand on his uniform before he held it out to Papa.

Papa shook his hand firmly. Sam looked over at the town square as if he was ready to flee. I slid my hand around his elbow. He glanced at me, and I smiled, hoping to bolster him.

Will, Hannah, and the rest of the Colters swarmed around us. I introduced each of them to my family.

"Amy, it's so good to meet you," Hannah said as she hugged my mama. Mama's eyes went wide for a moment, and then she hugged Hannah back.

"You have raised a lovely young woman in both character and beauty," she added.

My cheeks warmed under Hannah's praise.

"Thank you."

Hannah led Mama toward the town square, chatting all the way. The rest of us followed. Will asked my papa about his farm. Papa asked about the ranch. They seemed to get along well. Deacon and Grady formed an instant friendship, despite their three-year age difference.

It was almost lunchtime, so Hannah suggested we line up for the meal. Sam excused himself to change out of his uniform back at the boardinghouse. I fixed a plate for him so he could spend more time with me.

We split up between two different tables. I sat with my parents, Will, Hannah, and Violet. I saved a seat for Sam. Grady and the rest of the Colter boys sat far away from us.

When Sam joined us, I noticed he wore his suit, except for his jacket. He parted his damp hair to the side. His eyes lit with excitement when he saw me. He took a seat next to me.

"Don't you look dapper," I said.

"I hoped I wouldn't meet your parents in my uniform. Some first impression I gave."

I took his hand beneath the table and squeezed it. "Don't

worry. Just be yourself."

Sam listened intently to the conversation between our parents, but he said very little. Several times, he rubbed his hands on his legs and shifted his position.

I glanced at my watch pin. "Oh, my goodness! I need to go," I said as I stood. "I have an event for the newspaper at one. Hannah, are you still coming?"

She stood, and we walked away. Sam jogged up next to us.

"What's going on?"

"Come with us and see," I said.

Hannah and I took the stage as Clayton stood at the podium. He used a speaking trumpet to amplify his voice over the noise of the crowd.

"People of Prescott gather around!"

Sam moved to a spot near the front of the crowd. He looked at me with one eyebrow raised.

"You have followed the stories by E. M. Thatcher about the train accident and the now famous Mrs. Colter. We thought you might enjoy meeting both women."

The crowd murmured. Sam stood taller and smiled at me.

Clayton motioned for Hannah to stand next to him. "This is our very own Mrs. William Colter, the heroine of the train car derailment."

The crowd cheered as Hannah waved. They wanted her to say a few words, but she declined.

Then Clayton motioned me forward. "Today, I am pleased to introduce you all to Miss Ellie Mae Thatcher. You know her by her pen name, E. M. Thatcher."

I smiled and waved as I stepped forward. The crowd slowly clapped as they realized the reporter that they fell in love with was a woman. It felt good to stand before them and receive their appreciation.

"Miss Thatcher and Mrs. Colter will sign a special edition of the Prescott Gazette today. Please form a line and get your dimes ready!"

I led Hannah over to the table. I motioned for Sam to join us.

"Surprise!" I said to him as he kissed me on the cheek. "I guess your sweetheart and your mama are famous now."

He smiled and squeezed my hand. "I'm so proud of you. I'll leave you to your fans."

"Not so fast," Hannah said. "You get the first copy." She quickly signed her name by the Rancher's Wife article. I sign-ed my name across the top of the newspaper with a special note just for Sam. He leaned down and kissed me on the cheek before he faded into the crowd.

I looked forward to seeing him later in the afternoon.

James Colter appeared before me. "Mama. Ellie Mae."

He gave his mother a kiss on the cheek. Then he looked at me. "Can I talk to you for a minute?"

I stood and moved a few paces away.

"I really need you to run that article like we talked about." He looked over his shoulder. Then he rubbed the back of his neck.

"What's going on, James?" I asked.

His eyes danced from the stage to his mother to me. "Things are getting worse at the railroad. We need some publicity. I'm concerned about... I can't say more."

"I'll speak to my editor again," I promised. "He doesn't like the idea of me writing an article at your request."

"Please, Ellie Mae. I really need this."

I nodded and returned to my seat. As I signed more news-papers, I couldn't shake the feeling that James was in over his head.

CHAPTER 29

SAM

While Ellie Mae signed newspapers for her fans, I walked around the festival. I spotted Deacon, Grady, and Preston watching a cowboy tame a bronco.

"Someday, I'm gonna do that," Preston said.

"Not as long as Mama is alive," Deacon said.

I snorted.

"Is it hard?" Grady asked.

"I've done it before with some of the wild horses Uncle Adam trained."

My eyes went wide. Mama could not know about that. He was only sixteen, almost seventeen. Too young for something so dangerous.

James came up beside me.

"Wasn't sure if we'd see you," I said. "Too busy for the family?"

"Leave off it, Sam. I have a lot on my mind."

I frowned. "What is going on with you?"

"Do you really want to know?" He pulled me away from the rest of my brothers.

I narrowed my eyes and straightened my back.

"I need to get rid of my stake in the railroad. To do that,

I need Ellie Mae to print her interview. The longer she waits, the more trouble it makes for me. I need you to convince her to write it."

I pressed my lips into a thin line. "I will not do that."

"Please, Sam."

I crossed my arms. James never begged me for anything. Desperation clouded his eyes.

"Leave her out of this."

"Nothing will happen to her if she writes it. It's the last piece I need to fall into place."

I stepped closer to him and let my arms fall to my sides. "Don't drag her into your problems. If you do, you will answer to me."

James raised his hands, showing me his palms as he backed away. "I thought you had my back."

He turned on his heel and stormed away.

"What was that about?" Deacon asked me.

"Never mind."

I walked away from the cowboy tournament to find Ellie Mae.

"Sam!" She found me. "Look at this game. You throw a baseball at a stack of bottles. If you knock them all down, you win a prize."

Her eyes lit with excitement. "Win me something."

I smiled. "Alright."

I paid the nickel for two tries, but only needed the one. The man behind the counter offered a choice of candy to Ellie Mae. She chose the taffy.

"Ith thicky," she said. The candy stuck to her teeth. "Want thum?"

I laughed. "No, thank you. Looks like you're enjoying it."

She winked at me.

As we walked, I took her hand and laced my fingers with hers. I could spend forever walking by her side. We stopped to watch some couples compete in the three-legged race. I blew out a breath. Thankfully she didn't want to race either. I could not imagine her father's annoyance if we had.

The festivities wound down. Ellie Mae joined my family for supper when I left for supper with her parents.

I was a nervous wreck as I approached the boardinghouse. I hated I met Ellie Mae's parents in my baseball uniform, all dusty that morning. It was not the impression I hoped to make.

Since that greeting, I felt out of sorts. I was a little frightened of Mr. Thatcher. He had the power to bless my relation-ship with Ellie Mae or to end it.

I swallowed hard and checked my neck scarf. I smoothed a hand down the front of my vest. Then I opened the door.

Millie Lancaster greeted me with a smile and led me to a private dining area where Mr. and Mrs. Thatcher sat. I wished Ellie Mae was with me.

"Sam," Mr. Thatcher greeted me.

"Mr. Thatcher. Mrs. Thatcher."

"Please call us Lee and Amy," Mrs. Thatcher said.

I nodded as I took the seat that Lee pointed to. Ellie Mae was the spitting image of her father. Same sandy brown hair and nutmeg eyes. Only hers did not narrow when looking at me. Amy was thin with sandy brown hair and dark chocolate brown eyes. Grady favored his mother.

Millie brought in three plates. Then she closed the door be-hind her.

"Tell us about yourself," Lee said after he blessed the meal.

I took a gulp of water. Perspiration dotted my forehead as the air warmed. I told them about my work and a little about my family.

Lee's gaze pierced through me the whole time. Amy was much friendlier than her husband. She asked me several questions. When I looked at her, I felt more at ease. She had a grace about her, like Ellie Mae.

When the main part of the meal was over, Lee narrowed his eyes. "So, you intend to marry her?"

I fidgeted with the dessert fork. "Only if you give your blessing."

"And if I don't?"

I looked at the closed door to the room, unable to meet his gaze. "Then as difficult as it would be," I coughed. "I would find some way to extract her from my heart but there would not be much of it left."

My gaze traveled to Amy first. She smiled and rested a hand over her heart. Lee frowned.

"You only just met her."

"Yet, I feel like I've known her for a lifetime."

I pushed my dessert plate away, untouched.

"Lee," Amy whispered. "Don't be so hard on him."

"Amy." His tone warned her to silence.

Lee continued, "Even though she is independent and headstrong, she needs a man who will provide for her. She might not always have a career. This could be a passing fan-cy."

I wasn't sure if he meant me or her job.

"I will think about it and send you my answer soon."

"Thank you, sir."

"It was nice meeting you," Amy said.

I took that as my sign to leave. I stood and shook Lee's hand as a vise gripped my stomach. Even though I wanted to honor Ellie Mae's father, if he did not give his blessing, I was not sure I could let her go. With head hung low, I left the most awkward dinner of my life behind.

When I stepped onto the porch, Ellie Mae waited for me.

"How did it go?"

I shook my head. "He said he will send me his answer in the mail."

She frowned. "I don't know why he is being so difficult. I am going to talk to him."

She turned to go inside. I grabbed her arm and pulled her to me.

"Ellie Mae, let your father decide what he will."

I leaned down and gave her a quick kiss.

"I need to go. I'll see you soon?"

She nodded slowly.

"Promise me you won't pester him."

"I promise."

Then I found the rest of my family and we headed home. A scant part of my heart tried to prepare for the coming rejection.

The next few weeks were tough. I spent some time with Ellie Mae, but I avoided kissing her. Our conversation stilted. She felt distant. I feared I might lose her.

Week after week, no word came from her father. I hoped his silence was not his answer. I could not bear the thought of a lifetime without Ellie Mae.

CHAPTER 30

ELLIE MAE

The morning of July fifth, I met my family in the boarding-house's parlor to say my farewells.

I asked my parents what they thought about Sam.

"He clearly loves you very much," Mama said. "He seems to have your best interests in mind."

"Amy," Papa warned. "Don't get her hopes up. I told him I would send my decision in a letter."

Then Mama argued with Papa, something I had never seen.

"Lee, he is a good match for Ellie Mae. She is for him. It is plain as day when they are together. His family speaks highly of him. Just because you aren't ready for your daughter to marry doesn't mean she's not ready."

I bit my tongue to keep from adding to what Mama said.

"It is my decision. I will give an answer when I am ready."

"Papa, we love each other," I pleaded. "He is a good man. I know he's quiet, but I like that about him. He is dependable. Goodness, he came to find me when the train derailed, and he brought me back to Prescott safely. What else do you need to know?"

"Enough! Leave me be."

My eyes burned. Mama gave me a hug and whispered so only I could hear, "Give him a few weeks. I'll help him come around."

I stiffly hugged my papa and said goodbye to my brother.

My heart ached. I did not understand why Papa resisted the idea of a marriage between Sam and me. Clearly, Sam im-pressed Mama, and I had her blessing. But Sam would never move forward without Papa's blessing. It made no sense why Papa withheld it.

Over the following weeks, I saw little of Sam. He usually came to town on Tuesday or Wednesday and had lunch with me. He was busy at the ranch dealing with health issues among the stock. After a heavy monsoon season, some cattle developed black foot. They lost about twenty head of the one- to two-year-olds before they could isolate the infected animals.

I missed him terribly. I wished I could move back to the cabin at the ranch just so I could see him. Or that my father would write back and give Sam permission to marry me.

I settled into a routine at the Gazette. When I arrived in the morning, I typed up articles from interviews the previous day.

I worked on a series about the railroad, which included periodic updates on the reopening of the line. It took until the third week of July to complete the repairs. One article detailed the internal conflict that James Colter and Frank Murphy told me about. When I wrote it, Clayton decided it was worth printing, and it did not feel like either man influenced it.

After four weeks with no word from my papa, I resisted

the temptation to go home to speak with him. He was being unreasonable. His lack of response became a source of tension between Sam and me. We both needed some resolution.

Then, on August tenth, I received a letter. The postmark was from Chino Valley, but the return address was not my home. It was from our neighbor.

Dear Ellie Mae,

I regret to inform you that both of your parents were murdered last week. Grady is safe and staying with us.

Your father was working out in the field when a band of rustlers rode through the farm, destroying some crops. They shot your father in cold blood. When your mother went to investigate the sound of the gunshot, they shot her as well. Fortunately, Grady was not injured.

By the time you receive this, we will have already had the funeral. I am sorry that the sheriff did not notify you sooner. I was furious when I discovered no one notified you.

Your father's attorney suggests you come home for a period to settle the affairs of your parents' estate and to collect Grady. He is furious and needs you more than ever.

Regards,

Mrs. Hallstead

All the air left my lungs. I staggered to the closest familiar place, the newspaper office. I sank down onto one chair in the lobby. My limbs felt numb. My head throbbed.

Then a strangled wail escaped from the depths of my soul. The activity in the newsroom quieted. Clayton came over and took the letter from my numb fingers. He sat next to me for a few minutes until he coaxed me across the street to the boardinghouse.

Millie sat with me for a long time as I cried uncontrollably.

"I need to see Sam," I said. "He'll know what I should do."

After I said so for the third time, Millie flew into action. She packed my things and had Paul fetch the wagon. They thought I should stay with the Colters during my mourning because I was so close to Sam.

The trip to the ranch barely registered, as I was in so much shock. My parents were dead. I had to care for Grady. I had to determine what was to be done with our farm, our crops, our home. My stomach hurt. I felt woozy but it calmed.

When I arrived at the ranch, Sam was not at the house. Hannah led me directly into the parlor. She suggested I lay down on the couch for a few minutes. I heard Paul talk to her in muted tones. Then he left.

Hannah spoke to me softly. "Ellie Mae, I'm going to send someone to fetch Sam. Then I will be right back. I've set some water on the end table if you want it."

I thanked her and stared up at the ceiling. I was an orphan. It was a strange thought. I was eighteen and had a career and income. Wasn't an orphan someone with no parents? Grady was definitely an orphan.

A sob escaped my throat. Based on the date of the letter, Grady stayed with the Hallsteads for two weeks. He faced my parents' funeral alone.

Did Grady find them?

The thought made my stomach lurch. I stood and ran out-side. As I leaned over the railing of the porch, I heaved. I wail-ed as if hearing the news for the first time.

"Ellie Mae?"
Sam. Sweet blessed Sam. I collapsed into his arms.

CHAPTER 31

SAM

The morning of August tenth, I headed out to the herd. Papa, Deacon, and I worked with the local vet, Ray Sawyer, to deal with the outbreak of black foot. We saw no fresh signs of infection among the youngest cattle of the herd in over a week. Ray thought we were in the clear. Our total losses were thirty-five head by then.

When Ray headed back toward town, I saw a rider coming toward us. As he closed the distance, I recognized Uncle Adam. He came straight to me, not Papa.

"What is it?" I asked as he reined in the horse.

"It's Ellie Mae. You need to come now."

My stomach tightened as I mounted Bailey. "Where is she?"

"Ranch house."

I kicked Bailey into a gallop. Questions whirled around in my mind. What was she doing at the ranch? What happened? Was she alright?

Then I saw her on the porch as I closed the distance. She heaved over the railing.

I dismounted Bailey and tossed the reins in the general direction of a post before I hurried up the porch stairs.

"Ellie Mae?"

She looked frightfully pale. She turned to me, and her legs gave out. I caught her before she fell to the ground. Then I eased her onto a nearby rocking chair.

"Mama!" I hollered for her, frightened about what caused Ellie Mae to be in such a state.

"Sam! I'm here," Mama said as she brought some water for Ellie Mae.

I kneeled in front of Ellie Mae and clasped her hands. "Tell me what happened."

"My parents." Her voice broke and sobs cut off any more words.

I frowned. Did Lee Thatcher tell his daughter she couldn't marry me? If so, I was going to ride to Chino Valley and have words with him.

"Her parents were murdered," Mama said calmly. "Come, let's get her inside. You can read the letter."

Murdered.

The word hung in the air like a boulder perched on the edge of a cliff. Then it slammed into my heart with crushing weight. The breath left my lungs in a whoosh. I looked at Mama to make sure I heard correctly. The grimace on her face confirmed it.

I stood and placed my arm around Ellie Mae's waist as I helped her to her feet. Then I led her to a seat at the dining table before I sat next to her. Mama took a seat across from us.

"Drink some water," she said as she slid the glass toward Ellie Mae.

Ellie Mae complied.

"Sam, read this." Mama handed me the letter.

I read it twice as Ellie Mae pressed into my side. I rubbed my hand up and down her arm.

My eyes met Mama's.

"She needs you, Sam. She needs your help."

Papa and Deacon entered the room. Mama shook her head and rose to speak to them outside.

"Ellie Mae," I whispered. "Look at me."

I angled toward her so I could see her face. When she lifted her head, she looked a decade older than when I last saw her. Part of her hair came loose from the knot at the base of her neck. Her shirt held several wrinkles. Her pale face contrasted stark-ly with her red-rimmed eyes.

In that moment, I felt the soul-wrenching pain emanating from her. I guided her head to rest against my heart. Then I kissed the top of her head.

"I'll take you home. We'll leave tomorrow morning."

"Thank." She shuddered. "You."

I led her over to the couch in the parlor. She laid down.

"Sleep for a while. I'm here now."

When her eyes fluttered shut, I joined Papa, Deacon, and Mama in the dining room. I ran a hand through my hair. I stared at the stove in the kitchen. Someone murdered her par-ents.

"We'll leave in the morning," I said. "I'll take her home and help her through this."

"I'll come with you, son," Papa said.

"Oh, you're right. I can't go alone." The impropriety never crossed my mind. She needed me and I would be there.

"Deacon and Warren can handle any further issues with the herd," Papa said.

It occurred to me that Papa probably knew exactly what was involved in settling an estate, as he went through it when his papa died. I felt a small amount of relief knowing he would advise me and Ellie Mae.

The next morning, we left just after dawn. I drove the wagon as Ellie Mae clung to me. Papa rode Nugget, and he led Bailey behind him. I needed my horse while we were there and for the trip back.

Worry tried to fight its way into my mind. What if she wanted to stay and run the farm? Should I marry her and stay with her?

The thought of becoming a farmer made my skin crawl. I knew nothing about farming. I was a rancher, a cattleman.

For the first time in my life, I realized I belonged at the ranch. I was a third-generation cattleman. It was in my blood. The things I neglected to learn about the cattle growing up, I spent the last several months learning. The smell of the cattle made me feel good. I knew how to run the ranch. I was good at it. Since my birthday, it was no longer just *the* ranch; it was *my* ranch.

I placed my arm around Ellie Mae. She fell asleep against my side. She was the love of my life. I would do anything for her, but I hoped she would not ask me to become a farmer. It might be the one thing I would not do for her.

When we arrived at her home, she cried some more while Papa and I brought in our bags from the wagon.

Their home was much smaller than ours. It was a simple three-bedroom log cabin with one large open room with a parlor, dining, and kitchen area. A small desk stood at one end of the parlor. A couch and a few wingback chairs faced the fireplace.

The house smelled unpleasant. I found the source. Some rotten food sat in a pan. The waste pail stored more rotten food. I took them both outside and found the compost heap and dumped them on it.

When I returned, Ellie Mae turned her sad nutmeg eyes to-ward me.

"I can't believe they are gone."

"I know."

"I argued with Papa about you. My last words and feelings were anger."

She accepted my embrace. "He knows you loved him."

Papa opened some windows to air out the place.

"We should go pick up Grady from the Hallstead's house," she said.

"Alright. The team is still hitched to the wagon. We can go now."

She nodded.

Papa stayed behind to take stock of the provisions at their house.

Ellie Mae directed me towards the neighbor's house. I said a silent prayer that Grady fared well.

CHAPTER 32

ELLIE MAE

When we arrived at the Hallstead's, Sam helped me down from the wagon. I remembered our kind neighbors from church potlucks growing up.

"Ellie Mae," Mrs. Hallstead greeted me. "Please come in."

I introduced Sam.

"Your brother is still in his room. He comes out for meals, but has allowed no one in."

Mrs. Hallstead led me to the door. I took a deep breath to calm my nerves. Then I knocked on it.

"Go away!" Grady's voice was muffled by the door.

"It's me," I said.

I heard some movement. Then the door opened a sliver.

"Ellie Mae?"

I forced a smile to my face. "In the flesh."

He swung the door open wide and flung himself into my arms. I hugged him close. Then he sobbed, which made me break down.

After a few minutes, we settled down. He stepped back, and I studied him. His normally lanky body looked thinner than when I saw him a month ago. The dark shadows under his brown eyes aged him several years. He had grown a few more inches taller than me. He smelled like he needed a bath.

"I'm here to take you home."

He backed up a few steps. "I... I don't think I can go back there."

"You must. We must decide together what will become of our home."

He shook his head. He leaned forward like a coyote ready to pounce. His arm twitched.

"Grady, please. I can't do this without you. It's time we face things and move forward."

He glared at me but followed me as I headed out the door.

Sam asked Mrs. Hallstead about Grady's things. He gathered them from the room before he joined us outside.

"It was awful, Ellie Mae," Grady whispered as he climbed into the back of the wagon. "I saw them kill Mama."

As tears trickled down my cheeks, I sucked in a deep breath of air. "I'm so sorry, Grady. I'm sorry I did not come sooner."

Sam placed his arm around me. Then he drove us home. The closer we got; the more agitated Grady became.

"Don't look at where it happened," Sam suggested. "Just take deep breaths. Focus on the front door of the house."

When Grady calmed, I whispered to Sam, "Thank you."

Grady darted into the house, then he yelled.

"It's alright son," Will's voice came from inside. "I'm Sam's Papa. We met in Prescott, remember?"

Sam helped me down from the wagon and we both hurried inside.

"Deep breaths," Sam said.

Grady calmed down and Will led him to a chair. When he finally relaxed, Will suggested a bath. Grady complied.

As the day wore on, I grew more exhausted. It pained me to go through Mama and Papa's things. I did not know what to do. Nothing prepared me for such a task. I thought they would grow old and see both me and Grady married. I thought they would hug their grandchildren and laugh with joy over the silly things children said.

Will and Sam were godsends. Will cared for the barn animals. Seemed Mr. Hallstead had been coming over to care for them. Then he made us supper. I completely forgot about cooking and meals.

Sam helped me sort through things and offered hugs, encouraging smiles, and comfort in so many ways.

After a solemn supper, I started going through the papers on Papa's desk. An envelope addressed to Sam caught my attention. I called to him.

He took the envelope from me. "He wrote after all."

My gaze connected with Sam's. "If it is bad news, I can't bear to hear it."

Sam opened the letter and scanned it. "You'll want to hear this. I promise."

I sighed. "Go ahead."

"Dear Sam, I am sorry I was hard on you when we were in Prescott. I was not ready to admit my little girl grew up and was ready for marriage. Clearly, she is. Her heart has chosen you."

"What more could a father hope for than a dependable…"

Sam coughed.

"A dependable, loving son-in-law for his precious girl."

Tears streamed down my face at my father's admission.

"It would be my and Amy's honor to welcome you into

our family. You have my blessing to ask Ellie Mae to be your wife. I'm confident she will say yes."

Sam's eyes teared up.

"Let us know when the wedding is so we can be part of the celebration."

His voice cracked. I stood and put my arms around his middle. His arms encircled me with warmth and love.

"I'm so sorry my last words to him were in anger," I cried.

"Shh."

Sam rubbed his hand on my back. Will shuffled his feet.

"It's getting late," Will said. "We'll stay in the barn."

"Oh, no," I said. "Please, make use of the other bedroom." I couldn't bring myself to call it my parents' room anymore.

"I'll sleep on the floor," Sam volunteered. "Good night, Ellie Mae."

Grady was already asleep in his room when I checked on him. He snored softly, so I went to bed.

The next day, the four of us met with the attorney. My parents left the farm to Grady and me. We signed some paper-work. Then we left and purchased food at the mercantile.

When we arrived home, it was time for an honest conversation with my brother.

"Grady, we need to decide what to do with this place."

"What do you mean 'do with it'? We're going to harvest what's left and plant again next spring," he said.

As I looked away, I said, "I have a job in Prescott. I'm going back."

He frowned and slammed a fist down on the table. "So, you're gonna leave me to do this by myself?"

"I…"

"Ellie Mae, Grady," Sam whispered. "It might be best if you hire some tenants to farm. You could give them a per-cent-age of the harvest. Let them stay in the house. Grady could move to Prescott with us."

"What do you mean?" I asked.

"Papa and I talked it over last night. Grady could live at the ranch with me and my brothers. He got along well with Deacon. Maybe they could share a room. You could move back into the cabin. For now."

My cheeks warmed at the tender way he said it.

"Hannah and I would love to have you both," Will said. "If you'd rather be independent, there is the old ranch house that Hannah and I first lived in years ago—Julia and Adam's place. They moved into one of the larger homes on the property."

I blinked. Grady stared at the tabletop.

"We'll give you a few minutes to talk it over," Sam said, "while we see to the animals."

The two of them left. I sighed heavily and looked over at my brother.

So many emotions crossed his face. Anger. Grief. Pain. Sadness. I felt it all and more.

"I can decide for us, if you'd like," I said. "I don't want to force you to do something you don't want to."

"I miss them, Ellie Mae."

Tears rolled down my face. I grew weary of crying but fail-ed to stop it. "So do I."

I wiped away my tears as I waited for him to speak again.

"I can't farm by myself," he said. "I don't want to sell it. Not yet. I might want to come back when I'm older."

"Then we should find renters, like Sam suggested. He's very good with business and financial matters. I'm sure he can help us figure that out."

He rubbed his hand over a spot on the tabletop. "What's it like on the ranch?"

For the first time in days, I felt genuinely excited. "You will love it there. It's so beautiful. Hannah is the sweetest woman. I felt like I was part of the family when I was there to interview her. Sam's brothers are quite a handful, but Deacon and Preston are close to your age. Will is patient and kind. He's a good leader. And you already know that I think Sam walks on water."

He snorted.

"I suppose it makes sense for me to finish school and start thinking about my future. Sounds like a good place to do it."

"So, you want to come with me to Colter Ranch?" I asked.

"Yes."

"Do you want to room with Deacon? Or we could live in the cabin?"

"Come on, Ellie Mae. It's you and Sam that are gonna have your own place. Not you and me."

My face warmed when I noticed Sam in the kitchen. I missed hearing him and Will come back in. I wondered how much he heard.

"Then it's settled. As soon as we get the affairs in order here, we'll move to Colter Ranch."

Over the next week, we finished going through Mama and Papa's things. Sam and the attorney developed a plan to entice tenants to manage the farm for the next few years until Grady decided if he wanted to come back or not. The attorney agreed to vet and choose the tenants and to hire someone to care for the farm in the short-term. They presented a plan to Grady and me. We agreed and signed the paperwork.

CHAPTER 33

SAM

Two weeks later, it was our last morning in Chino Valley at the Thatcher farm, and it went by fast. We cleaned up the house and packed up the things that Ellie Mae and Grady planned to bring with them. Grady preferred to drive the wagon with Ellie Mae by his side.

I mounted Bailey. Papa and I rode ahead of the wagon.

"Thank you for coming," I said to Papa.

Papa nodded. After several minutes, he said, "I'm very proud of you, Sam. Your idea of bringing them back to the ranch and leasing out their farm was smart."

My chest puffed up as I tried to accept the praise.

"You cared for your woman in a troublesome time."

I rested my hand on the saddle horn. Seemed like Papa had more to say.

"I was relieved when Ellie Mae found the letter from her father. If you did not have his blessing, I worried you would let her slip away. That would have been a mistake. A love like what you two have. Well, it's a precious thing. A gift from the Almighty."

I looked over my shoulder at Ellie Mae. She waved. I nodded.

Papa was right. I loved her from the depths of my soul. In her, God made the perfect woman for me. Smart. Kind. Loyal. Charming. In a few short months, she won my heart, started a friendship with my mama, and earned Papa's respect. She saved Mama's life. Violet looked up to her. Even my brothers thought highly of her. She belonged at the ranch as a part of our family.

"Any advice on how to propose?" I asked.

Papa laughed. "You'll figure it out."

"I suppose I should talk to Mama and enlist her help."

"I'm sure Vi would help, too."

I nodded.

"You should set Ellie Mae up in Aunt Julia's old house. It makes sense if you're gonna marry her, she should move in there now. Save you the trouble of moving her twice."

A part of me wanted her to return to her cabin instead of the larger old ranch house, not that it was much larger. The two-bedroom home had a large open kitchen, dining room, and parlor. When Aunt Julia lived there, she and Adam gave their three girls the larger bedroom and they took the smaller room. I wanted that larger bedroom for me and Ellie Mae. Once we had a family, we would figure out how to manage.

My faced warmed at the thought.

The rest of the trip passed in silence. We arrived home before suppertime. Deacon and Preston helped unpack Ellie Mae and Grady's things from the wagon. We carried the furniture that Ellie Mae wanted to keep to the old ranch house.

"Wait, I'm moving in here?" Ellie Mae asked.

"It's bigger," I said. I took her hands in mine. "It will be our home when we marry."

She smiled and looked away. It was too soon to ask her

properly. She needed time to grieve the loss of her parents.

"I will need my typewriter brought here. Since I'll be far from the office, I will only want to go into town a few days a week. Hopefully, Clayton will approve that."

"I am sure he will be. You're one of his best journalists."

She walked into the home. She ventured into the kitchen and opened a few cupboards. Then she closed them again.

"The hutch can go over here." She pointed to a place along the wall of the dining room. "I'll put Mama's dishes in it."

She sniffed, and my heart broke. I did not want to imagine how I would feel when my mama passed. Hopefully, it would be decades from then.

Ellie Mae opened the doors to the bedrooms. "There's no furniture."

We did not bring any beds from the Thatcher farm since we wanted to leave them for the tenants.

"We'll move the bed over from the cabin. Table too. Until I can make a new one."

"Can you bring the dresser as well?"

I nodded. Deacon and Preston followed me. In the end, we brought over all the furniture from the cabin. In the coming weeks, I would get some furniture of our own.

Mama appeared in the doorway of the old ranch house. "It is time for supper."

She took Ellie Mae's arm and walked beside her. "How are you doing?"

I missed Ellie Mae's response as I hurried toward the water pump to wash off some of the dust from the trip and moving furniture.

When I sat down at the table, Ellie Mae already sat at the foot of the table. I let out a long breath. She was home.

I took my seat next to her. Vi offered her seat to Grady, but he took a seat next to me and across from Deacon.

After Papa prayed for the meal, the conversation started.

"I was thinking," Papa said, "We can put Preston in with Boone. Deacon and Grady can share a room. Since James bought a house in town, Sam can have his old room."

"That would be nice," Mama agreed. "Grady, does that sound good to you?"

Grady nodded. He shifted in his chair. When Deacon start-ed a conversation with him, he seemed to relax.

I glanced over at Ellie Mae. Her eyebrows drew togeth-er. I took her hand and squeezed.

"Give it some time," I whispered.

After supper, Ellie Mae said she was tired, so I walked her over to the old ranch house. She turned to face me. I rested my hands on her hips, and she slid her arms around my neck.

"Thank you, Sam, for everything. For being my rock. For figuring out the wisest plan."

I smiled down at her. Words stuck in my throat. Her nut-meg eyes searched mine. I looked at her lips.

"Can I kiss you?"

She surprised both of us when she drew my head down towards her. Her lips felt soft as she pressed them against mine. As I parted my lips, my hands moved from her hips to her back, and I pressed her closer, delighting in the feel of her against me. Her arms held me tight. When I deepened the kiss, she matched my intensity. Love and desire compet-ed within me. I wanted her. Only her.

When she placed a hand on my chest, my blood boiled. Then she leaned back. Space separated our lips. As I fought to breathe normally again, I rested my forehead on hers.

"I love you, Ellie Mae."

"You know I love you back."

I smiled.

"You should probably let me go before your Mama sends one of your little brothers out here to ruin the moment."

She nodded toward the kitchen window. I looked that way. Sure enough, Mama and Papa kept a watchful eye.

"I could give them a show," I teased.

She stepped away from my embrace. "Some other night. I feel like I haven't slept in days."

As I turned to leave, she added, "Can you make sure my brother gets some rest? I'm worried about him."

"Yes, ma'am."

She snickered.

I turned back toward her and raised an eyebrow.

"Oh, I just remember you saying that the day we met. It seemed natural for you to say ma'am. Yet, it also seemed like it didn't belong with your fancy suit and bowler hat."

I grinned. "I can see how you thought that. You can put that in your book."

"Alright. I'm going now," she said. But she didn't move.

I heard the soft click of the door latch behind me as I turned and walked to the house. Soon enough I would make her my wife.

CHAPTER 34

ELLIE MAE

"Morning," Sam greeted me as I stepped out of the old ranch house two weeks later.

I wanted to think of it as our house, but I refused to let myself until Sam proposed. Which he still had not done.

I kissed him on the cheek and took his arm as he led me over to the big house for breakfast.

"I have something for you."

I smiled as my heart hoped it was a ring.

"Wait until after breakfast."

He held the door open. Then he held out a chair for me at the foot of the table.

After Will blessed the meal, Deacon and Grady chatted about Deacon's new job with the vet.

"Can I leave school if Deacon gets called out for Mr. Wil-son's pregnant goat?" Grady asked. "I want to see the babies born."

It seemed foreign to me to grant or deny permission for my younger brother. I was only four years older.

"If you can make up your schoolwork, then yes," I said.

Grady grinned from ear to ear. He seemed interested veterinary medicine like Deacon. I wondered if he might pursue something similar when he finished school.

My worrying heart felt relieved that his grief lifted. I knew it wasn't gone. Mine certainly wasn't. We both were learning how to move on from the loss of our parents.

Hannah glanced at the clock on the wall. "You need to get going to school."

Grady swallowed his last bite of food. Violet grabbed her empty plate and set it in the sink. Preston downed the last of his coffee. They headed out to the barn.

"Come on," Sam said as he grabbed my hand. "I want Grady to be here when I give my surprise to you."

I smiled and hurried beside him. He spoke often of us and our future. I wondered if he was about to ask me at last. I hoped so.

Deacon saddled his horse while Grady and Preston readied the wagon. Dory joined Violet and hopped into the back of the wagon.

"Wait here," Sam said. He went into the barn. He was gone for a few minutes before he returned with a white horse.

"Ellie Mae," he said, "meet your horse, Moonlight."

I quickly masked my disappointment as I told myself that a horse was no small gift. I forced a smile.

"You bought me a horse?"

"And a sidesaddle."

"I helped pick out the mare," Grady said. "I thought you would like her."

"She's lovely."

I let Moonlight smell my hand. Then I rubbed her face. When I felt like we were friends, I moved my hand along her neck as I walked beside her. The sidesaddle looked expensive. It was more ornate than the plain one I rented from the livery.

Sam stood beside me. "I had your initials added here."

He pointed to the letters. "E. M." No last initial.

"Thank you," I said as I tried to keep a positive perspective. It really was a wonderful gift. It just wasn't the gift I want-ed the most.

The rest of the family headed off to town. Sam led me and Moonlight toward the old ranch house.

"Now you can go to town whenever you want. She is very gentle and won't give you any trouble."

I smiled as he looped the reins over the post by the old ranch house. Sam pulled me close.

"Grady told me today is your birthday."

Then he gave me a chaste kiss before he released me.

"You need to leave too," he said.

I went inside the house and grabbed my satchel. Then I returned to where my new horse stood. Sam gave me a leg up.

"Have a good day, Ellie Mae."

I thanked him again and pointed Moonlight toward town.

Once I was out of sight, I let my tears fall. My emotions churned. I missed my parents. It was my first birthday without them.

The sheriff never caught the men who murdered them. It took several years before a strange twist of fate led Grady and Deacon to find the killers. But that was their story to tell.

I loved Sam and his extravagant gift, but my heart ached over the lack of a proposal. I felt stuck between my old life and my hope for a new life with Sam. Once he asked me and we moved forward, my heart would heal more from the loss of my parents. Until then, I needed to figure out how to live in the in-between and stop driving myself crazy, anticipating a proposal.

I wiped the tears from my face.

"You're a good girl, Moonlight."

She snorted but kept a steady pace toward town.

By the time I arrived at the newspaper office, my emotions settled.

"Miss Thatcher?" one paperboy greeted me.

"Yes."

"Mr. Colter asked that whenever you come to town, I should take your horse over to Paul Lancaster's for the day. You can pick her up from there if I'm not around."

I thanked him and smiled. Sam arranged every detail.

I entered the newspaper office and walked to my desk. I halted when I saw a typewriter on it. My typewriter was at home.

After setting my satchel down, I ran my fingers lightly on the keys. It was a newer model and a different brand from mine. There was a piece of paper loaded like someone had already used it. I pulled out the page.

> By now, you are probably thinking I have spent too much on your birthday, between the horse, the saddle, and this.

My cheeks warmed and tears threatened to spill over. It was a note from Sam.

> You are worthy of such indulgences. Such gifts seem insignificant compared to how you have changed my life for the better.

> I wish gifts could take away the pain I know you feel today over the loss of your parents. Know I pray for you daily that in time your heart will heal, and you will be ready for the next adventure life will bring.

Happy birthday, dear love.

I held back the tears. I loved his acknowledgement of my grief. It occurred to me he held back a proposal to give my heart time to mend.

"I see you found his gift," Clayton said.

I nodded as I folded the note and hid it away in my satchel.

"He dropped it off earlier this week, but he said I should hold it in my office for today. Something about it being your birthday?"

I laughed. "Yes, it is."

"Happy birthday. Now," he said as he rubbed his hands together, "I've got a new assignment for you."

When he finished explaining the assignment, I mapped out a plan and set up interviews for the following week. Then I finished working on another article.

The day flew by. The paperboy who greeted me that morning let me know he had my horse saddled and ready to go. He helped me up, and I rode Moonlight home.

When I arrived home, Sam waited to help me down.

"I missed you," he said.

I laughed. "I've only been gone a few hours."

He gave me a roguish grin before he took Moonlight into the barn and brushed her down. I followed him.

"Thank you for the typewriter and the note."

He paused while brushing Moonlight.

"Are you alright? I know today must be hard."

He finished caring for the mare before I responded.

"I'm fine. It's weird. I figured my parents would miss this birthday because I lived in a different town from them, not because they were gone."

My voice cracked.

Sam took me in his arms and let me cry against his chest,

comforting me by rubbing small circles on my back. When I calmed, I leaned back to look into his eyes.

"I needed that."

He smiled. "Any time."

Then he released me and held my hand as we walked to the ranch house.

The rest of my birthday filled me with joy. Hannah made me a cake. Each of the Colters and Grady bought me gifts. I felt like part of the family.

CHAPTER 35

SAM

Almost two weeks after Ellie Mae's birthday, while she was in town working at the newspaper office, my family helped me transform the old ranch house. Boone and Deacon moved all the furniture from Ellie Mae's cabin back there. Then we unloaded a wagon full of new furniture, including a new bed, dressers, nightstands, parlor furniture, and end tables.

Papa and I handcrafted two tables. One was a smaller table for Ellie Mae's typewriter. We placed that in the parlor below the window that looked out toward the lake. The new dining table and chairs were enough to seat eight. Anything larger would not fit in the space.

Mama stocked the cupboards with new pots, pans, and bakeware. She set the table for two with dishes Ellie Mae brought back from the farm. Then she placed a vase full of flowers in the center.

"She'll love it," Mama said as she adjusted a few of the flowers. "What time is she due home?"

"Five o'clock. She promised," I said.

"Alright. I can bring your supper over around half past four and set it on the stove to warm. It should be fine."

"Thank you, Mama."

"We'll be expecting you for dessert by six. If you're late, I'm gonna send Boone to come in and fetch you." Her eyes held a soft warning.

"Yes Mama."

After my family left, I rearranged a few things. Then load-ed a sheet of paper in the typewriter for later.

No longer would I walk Ellie Mae here and leave her at the end of a long day. This would be our home.

My pulse raced as I pictured Ellie Mae there with me, sitting in the chairs gazing into the fire. I would read a dime novel to her. She would hold my hand. Our children's laughter would fill the room. One day she would finish her novel at the small table overlooking the lake, and I would celebrate with her when it was published. So many glorious memories awaited us. A lifetime together just might be long enough.

After one last look around, I closed the door behind me, satisfied that my plan came together.

CHAPTER 36

ELLIE MAE

When I arrived back at the ranch, Sam greeted me. He asked me to wait for him while he cared for Moonlight, so I did.

"Ready?" I asked as he joined me.

As he ran a hand through his hair, he smiled nervously. Then he held my hand and led me toward the ranch house. Before we made it to the front porch, he veered toward the old ranch house instead.

"I thought we ought to drop off your things."

He cleared his throat.

"Alright." His odd behavior made me antsy.

Then he opened the door and held it for me. The smell of roast beef greeted me. On the table sat two place settings and a vase of flowers.

Wait. It was a different table. I walked over and ran my hand along the polished cherry wood.

"Sam, what's going on?"

"I made a few changes while you were gone."

I snorted. "A few?"

I looked around the room. Everything was different. A new couch, two wingback chairs, and several side tables stood in the parlor. My typewriter rested on a new table in front of my favorite window. A fire glowed in the hearth.

Curiosity led me to the bedroom. A new, larger bed stood centered along one wall. Two dressers. Two nightstands.

My heart thudded rapidly in my chest. Two.

He took my hand and led me to the dining room table. Then he retrieved two plates from the stove.

"Mama made this, of course. But I thought it might be nice for us to share a quiet supper."

He held out a chair for me. I sat stunned by the transformation in the house. Then he sat across from me. When he finished blessing the meal, I still found no words.

I stared at him.

He smiled. "Eat up."

I ate a bite of food.

"It was about time we furnished the place instead of using that old rickety stuff from the little cabin. Do you like it?"

We. Two.

I wanted to hope.

"It's very nice. I love the dining table and the little table for my typewriter."

"I made those. With Papa's help."

"When did you find time?"

He laughed. "Ever since I gave you a horse, I had more time on my hands."

We bantered throughout the meal.

When I finished, he stood and came around the table. Then he took my hand.

"I have one more thing to show you."

He led me over to the typewriter. Then he sat down and typed something.

"Take a peek," he said as he went down on one knee.

My breath lodged in my throat. I lifted the carriage to see the words: Will you marry me?

Then I looked at him. He held out a ring.

I set the carriage down and then typed: Shift. Y. Shift. E. Shift. S.

He smiled and humored me. He stood and lifted the carriage.

Once he read my reply, he placed the ring on my finger. Then he drew me into his arms. My heart raced as I looped my arms around his neck and his lips captured mine. Tingles coursed through my body as I kissed him back with all the love of my heart. His hands roamed over my waist and back sending delightful shivers up my spine. Then he trailed kisses along my neck. I groaned before he captured my lips with his again.

A knock sounded at the door, and he abruptly released me, leaving me to miss his closeness.

"We better go," he said in a husky tone. He cleared his throat. "I promised Mama that I would have you up to the house for dessert by six. We're late. Oh, and I'll get your last initial, 'C', added to your saddle soon."

He winked at me.

I took his arm as Boone flung the door open.

"Come on, you two lovebirds. I'm ready for some pie."

I laughed as we walked past Boone.

———

Six weeks later, Hannah helped me into my wedding dress. Though the dress was made with the special day in mind, it was perfect for work or church, too. The light green silk reflected the light. Ivory lace edged the low neckline and edges of the sleeves. She fixed my hair in ringlets cascading down my back. I glanced in the mirror.

"You look so beautiful," Violet said.

"Thanks, Vi." I felt beautiful.

Hannah kissed me on my cheek. "He's going to love it."

A knock sounded on the door. Violet let Grady in.

"Wow! Sis, is that you?" he teased.

Hannah and Violet left.

"You look amazing," he said seriously. "Mama and Papa would be proud." He looked away and swallowed hard.

I cleared my throat to hold my tears at bay.

"Thank you for agreeing to walk me down the aisle."

"Of course."

We stood in silence for another minute. Then he led me to the door.

When we stepped out into the midday light, the cool air felt good. The sun warmed my face. The pastor stood by the lake. Sam stood next to the pastor. His smile seemed tentative when he caught sight of me.

"I think he's gonna cry," Grady said.

"Stop it," I growled.

Then I smiled at Sam as Grady led me toward him. He was right. Sam cried. Just a little. Until I stood next to him.

We said our vows in front of the entire Colter clan, including Sam's aunts, uncles, and cousins. When the pastor introduced us, Sam drew me close for a sweet kiss.

I was glad that Sam returned my letter all those months ago, and that I won his heart and became his wife.

CHAPTER 37

SAM

My wedding day arrived. Ellie Mae was going to be my wife. My fingers struggled with the buttons of my shirt as I dressed. I wore the neck scarf James got me for my birthday, as I figured my wedding was a fancy enough affair.

I rubbed my sweaty palms on my pant legs, then donned the gray vest and jacket. It was my nicest suit, one that Ellie Mae complimented me on.

As I went downstairs to the parlor, I recalled the day I met her. How beautiful she looked. How I was instantly taken with her as I helped her down from her horse.

I smiled as I remembered how upset I was to learn that E. M. Thatcher was a woman. I was glad she hid that from us. She was right. We would not have invited her to the ranch had we known. Without her, my life would be empty.

I looked out the window to where the family gathered. She would be sad her parents were not there, but I hoped that my family would help fill that void.

"It's time," Papa said.

I cleared my throat. Then I followed him out of the house toward the lake.

From my vantage point at the front of the gathering, I saw Ellie Mae as she stepped out of our house. Love for her rose within me, so strong that my eyes clouded. She looked stuning in her new dress.

The wedding blurred for me. I said and meant every word of my vows to her, which only reinforced what my heart had decided months ago. I kissed her.

Then we celebrated surrounded by my family.

As the sun dipped below the horizon, I led my wife to our home. I opened the door. Someone had started a fire in the fireplace, and it cast a glow on Ellie Mae's long hair. She turned to me and smiled.

I closed the door and took her in my arms.

"I don't have a note for you tonight," I said. "I want to say it loud."

She looped her arms around my neck.

"I love you, Ellie Mae. You make me a better man. You are everything to me."

"I love you, Sam. I'm kinda glad you answered my letter and let me come to Colter Ranch."

I laughed. Then I wiggled my eyebrows.

"Enough words for now."

Then I led her to our room and showed her how much I loved her.

EPILOGUE

Colter Ranch, Arizona Territory
November 5, 1907

ELLIE MAE

As I finished setting out supper, Hannah helped Will hobble to the table. He was aging rapidly and struggled with stairs. Cold days were tough too.

Will still sat at the head of the table with Hannah at his side, like the first day I came to Colter Ranch over twenty years ago. The house belonged to Sam and me. Will, Hannah, and Violet moved into the old ranch house after the last of the Colter sons left home.

There were some different faces around the table twenty years later. My husband, Sam, sat at the foot. I sat next to him. Then our children's faces replaced those of Sam's brothers and sister. I looked at my oldest, Sterling. He was eighteen, the same age as when I arrived at the ranch. Brody, our seventeen-year-old, sat next to him. Our last boy, Riley, was almost fourteen. They sat across from me, while our daughters Ashley and Scarlett sat next to me. Ashley was fifteen and Scarlett was twelve.

That day was a special day. Sam and I celebrated our

twentieth anniversary. I remembered thinking when I first met Hannah and Will that I wanted a husband who loved me like they loved each other after twenty years. The memory made me smile. I had a husband who loved me even more than I could imagine.

After Sam said the blessing, the boys started grabbing food. It reminded me of Sam's brothers.

"You're smiling a lot this evening," he said as he took my hand.

"Just remembering when I first came to the ranch."

"That was long before you became a famous author." He winked at me.

"I'm hardly famous."

"I think twenty novels beg to differ."

He read every one of them out loud to his father, who absolutely loved each of my books.

The banter around the table warmed my heart. The child-ren talked about their day in school. We sent them to town, as I had no time to teach them with my strict writing schedule.

When supper ended, Ashley and Scarlett cleared the ta-ble. Then they brought out a cherry pie.

"Hannah, you didn't have to," I said.

"I know. But it's your anniversary, and it's Sam's favor-ite."

"Thank you."

After dessert, our children disappeared to the parlor with Hannah and Will. Sam remained seated. He unfolded a piece of paper and handed it to me.

I loved our tradition of typewritten notes to each other. An anniversary or birthday did not pass without the ex-change. Some years we gave each other notes on additional days, others we only had the key milestones to remember.

I read the note.

> Each year, your beauty grows. Your heart was forever bound to mine the day we met, the day a nervous young man lifted you down from your horse. Your eyes met mine, and I was a goner. My eyes only saw you. Had we no audience that day and I had I been a braver man back then, I would have kissed you.
>
> Through ups and downs, pain and joy, our love flourishes. I did not know what true love was back then. Not even the night I made you my wife.
>
> True love deepens and matures. It settles and rebuilds. It sup-ports and nourishes.
>
> On this, our twentieth anniversary, I can promise you this: I love you more with each passing day and as you teach me the meaning of true love through your selflessness and encouragement. Without you, I would not be the man that I am. I would not be a good father or even a good husband. It is your love and the love of our Father above that enables me to be the best man I can be.
>
> I look forward to twenty years and more with you, my love.

I stood and so did he. Then he pulled me into his arms and kissed me like we were in our twenties again.

"I have something else for you," he said. He went into the parlor and came back with a beautiful wooden box that had intricate scrollwork on the top.

"Did you make this?" I asked.

"Yes. It's for my notes to you. I noticed your old box was falling apart."

"Sam, this is beautiful."

I traced my fingers over the initials carved in the center

of the top of the box. E.M.C. I like that he used my married initials and not my pen name. I opened the box and there were all our notes.

My eyes misted as I pulled out his very first note to me when he tested out my old Remington 2. Then I read his next note.

"Do you have a box for the notes from me?" I asked.

He smiled. "I made a matching one. Would you like to see it?"

I nodded.

He ran upstairs to our room. Then he came back with it.

"It's beautiful too," I said. His box matched mine except for his initials.

He pulled out the note I gave him on his twenty-first birthday. "That was some year, wasn't it?"

I smiled. "You mean besides the fact that you met me, fell in love, and became part owner of the ranch?"

"And made you my wife."

"Read it to me," I said.

He did. Then he read another. Then I read one to him. After a while, Hannah and Will retired to their home, escorted by Sterling to make sure they made it safely.

Our other children went to bed. Still, Sam and I read our notes from each other. With each whispered note, we smiled and shared our favorite part about that note. By the time we finished, it was well past midnight.

"I have one more to add to your collection," I said.

I handed him the note which said:

To my reluctant cattleman,

My, how you have grown and changed over the years from that young man who did not know his place in the Colter

Family.

Gone is your reluctance, replaced by enthusiasm. Gone is your uncertainty, replaced by confidence. Gone is your anxiety, re-placed by peacefulness.

Now you are the rock, the center, the patriarch of the Colter Family, not only for our branch but also for your siblings and their families.

I am honored to be called your wife and to wear your name. I am grateful to be the one you chose to share your life with.

All my love,

Ellie Mae

Then my confident cattleman led me upstairs to celebrate our anniversary in private, with our hearts entwining even deeper.

Author's Note

While working on *Joy for Mourning* in the *Desert Manna Series*, I wrote a scene where Joshua Harrison sees Hannah Colter for the first time after eight years. Hannah had not chosen him but chose Will Colter instead. To drive home the contrast between what Hannah had and what Joshua wanted, I gave the Colters five sons. Those few sentences led to the vision for the *Colter Sons Series*.

I grew excited about writing several coming-of-age stories about the children of beloved characters from the *Prescott Pioneers Series*. My plan for years has been to follow the lives of the Colter clan, so this was finally the right opportunity at the right time.

I knew from the beginning that I would not tell the sons' stories in birth order. I sat down one day and wrote Chapter 1 for all five stories in one afternoon. I chose the first-person style because I wanted to bring a richer flavor to the characters and deeper point of view. It was also to provide me a challenge to grow my writing skills even more.

Prior to writing the series, I went back and reread the *Prescott Pioneers Series*. I had forgotten about the kidnapping in Book 4. It provided the catalyst to start the *Colter Sons Series* with Sam. I asked the question what would happen to a young man who had been kidnapped as a baby? How would it affect his personality, world view, and view of his place in his family? What if he learned about the kidnapping in a way that felt shocking to him? As I considered all those questions, I decided a female journalist would be the perfect disruption to his quiet life.

Once I decided on a journalist, I was pleasantly surprised to discover how long ago typewriters were used. There were some unusual styles in the 1870s to the early 1900s before the styles settled into something that resembles the typewriters that were eventually replaced by computer keyboards. The first two major styles were the understrike, like Ellie Mae's typewriter, and the ball style. The ball style literally looked like a ball with keys protruding from the top. In both cases, the typist could not see what they typed. I can't imagine how frustrating that had to be, especially after being spoiled with our modern spellcheck and autocorrect. Most early type-writers did not even have shift keys or punctuation. Crazy! I chose the Remington Type 2 because it felt the most familiar to a modern audience with a few differences that I could easily describe.

In *The Reluctant Cattleman*, I introduced the real-life drama of the railroad wars in Prescott. Thomas Bullock was the first to incorporate a railroad. It was called the Central Arizona Railway. He received a lot of money from bonds if he completed the railroad by December 31, 1886. That was a massive challenge since construction started in May 1886. To complete the deadline, he chose to run the rails through several washes. In Arizona, when monsoon storms arrive, flash flooding is commonplace, even today. So, his decision to run the rails through washes would have been controversial. He also chose some shoddy construction materials. His only advantage was a lack of competition. His poor choices eventually led to several accidents with loss of life and many legal battles.

A rival railroad tried to get off the ground. It was called the Arizona Central Railway and it was started by Nathan Oakes Murphy. His brother, Frank Murphy, was heavily involved.

The big player in the railroad industry was the Atlantic & Pacific (A&P). They completed the line across the 35th parallel in northern Arizona in 1882, roughly 70 miles north of Prescott. The A&P repeatedly tried to negotiate a merger between the Central Arizona Railway and the Arizona Central Railway. Eventually, a merger happened, and the railway changed their name to the Prescott & Arizona Central Railway. Bullock and the Murphy brothers did not get along, and Bullock eventually forced Nathan Oakes Murphy out. The railroad wars were far from over. I tell more of this story in the next two books in the *Colter Sons Series*.

The history behind the railroads from the A&P all the way down to Phoenix was full of drama. I was very fortunate to find a detailed, well-researched book by John W. Sayre that told the story in detail. I also found several books about the history of the A&P which eventually became the Atchison, Topeka, and Santa Fe railroad. One of my favorite sources ended up being a book written in the 1880s that described how railroads were constructed, managed, and maintained. It allowed me to give Boone and James Colter realistic involvement in the creation of a railroad in the *Colter Sons Book 2 and Book 3*.

Anyway, I hope you enjoyed Sam and Ellie Mae's story. Continue the story with Boone, in *The Roaming Adventurer*.

Karen Baney

Want More Arizona Territory Romance?

Get a FREE novella featuring characters connected to the Colter Sons series! Plus exclusive updates on new releases, special offers, and historical insights from the frontier.

Subscribe at: books.karenbaney.com/larson-christmas

ABOUT THE AUTHOR

Karen Baney is passionate about writing stories full of flawed characters. She enjoys weaving together stories of second chances, redemption, and overcoming personal trials. As a transplant to Arizona, she loves researching the state's history and finding ways to seamlessly incorporate real history and real settings into her novels. In addition to writing and speaking, Karen works as a Software Development Manager for a Christian ministry.

Her faith plays an important role both in her life and in her writing. Karen and her husband, Jim, make their home in Gilbert, Arizona, with their two dogs, Bella and Daisy. Both Jim and Karen are active at Rock Point Church in Queen Creek, Arizona.

Discover faith-laced stories with characters who feel like lifelong friends.

Visit www.karenbaney.com to discover more historical romance series set in the American West. Follow Karen's writing journey and get behind-the-scenes glimpses of her research adventures on social media.

Facebook:	@AuthorKarenBaney
X:	@karen_baney
Instagram:	@AuthorKarenBaney
BookBub:	Follow Karen Baney for new release alerts

BOOKS BY KAREN BANEY

Historical Western Romance

Prescott Pioneers Series:

Step back in time to the wild, untamed Arizona Territory where survival depends on grit, faith, and the courage to start over. Follow three pioneer families—the Andersons, Colters, and Larsons—as they risk everything for the promise of a new life in a land that demands both strength and hope.

A Dream Unfolding
A Heart Renewed
A Life Restored
A Hope Revealed
Hidden Prospects

Desert Manna Series:

Sometimes the most beautiful love stories bloom in the desert. Set in the growing frontier town of Prescott during the early 1870s, these tender romances follow women rebuilding their lives after heartbreak and the unexpected men who help them discover that second chances at love are worth the risk. Set in Prescott, Arizona between 1871 - 1873.

Beauty for Ashes
Joy for Mourning
Oaks of Justice

Colter Sons Series:

Power, legacy, and forbidden love collide in this sweeping family saga set in the Arizona Territory. The Colter ranch empire has weathered decades of frontier life, but now family secrets and buried betrayals threaten to destroy everything. As five brothers—and one resilient sister—navigate the treacherous waters of love, loss, and redemption, they must decide what's worth fighting for. Set in Prescott and other locations within the Arizona Territory in 1887 - 1906.

The Reluctant Cattleman
The Roaming Adventurer
The Railroad Magnate
The Resourceful Stockman
The Restless Wrangler
The Resilient Bride

Larson Sisters Series
Meet the next generation! These delightful novellas follow the three daughters of Adam and Julia Larson from the *Prescott Pioneers Series* as they navigate love, courtship, and finding their own happily ever afters in territorial Arizona in 1886 – 1894.

In Love at Christmas
In Love with the Rancher
In Love with the Horse Trainer

Contemporary Romance

Vargas Ranch Series:
Love is in the air at the Vargas Guest Ranch & Resort near Wickenburg, Arizona. Meet the Vargas family—five swoon-worthy brothers and their cousins who live by their family motto: "We do not deviate from the Lord's plan."

These rugged cowboys run a successful working ranch and luxury resort while navigating the rollercoaster of finding true love.

Falling for a Fake Cowboy
Falling for a Real Cowboy
Honeymoon with a Real Cowboy
Falling for a Shy Cowboy
Falling for a Bossy Cowboy
Falling for a Smart Cowboy
Falling for a Humbug Cowboy
Falling for a Devoted Cowgirl
Falling for a Pregnant Cowgirl
Falling for a Cowboy's Legacy

Steadfast Love Series:
The *Steadfast Love* series follows a close-knit group of friends as they navigate the beautiful mess of modern life in the Phoenix area—workplace drama, complicated families, and love that shows up when they least expect it. These contemporary romances blend emotional depth with authentic faith, reminding us that even when life unravels, God's love never does.

The Heart I Rescue (prequel)
The Air I Breathe

Will I make the honorable choice to protect her future?

I won't be bridled by anyone… or so I thought.

My name is Boone Colter, and all I ever wanted was to focus on my career as a surveyor. Build up my business. Explore the wilderness. Then I met her, and she lied to me, putting me in a difficult position. I ought to let her deal with the mess she made.

But Mama raised me to make honorable choices. If I do, are we gonna be stuck with each other until death do us part? Will that come sooner than I think?

Only thing I know for certain, 1890 will change my life in ways no one could have foreseen.

If you love emotionally rich Christian romance with rugged frontier grit...

Janette Oke meets Louis L'Amour. Mary Connealy meets Zane Grey.

The *Colter Sons* series blends heartfelt faith journeys, masculine coming-of-age arcs, and sweeping Arizona history into unforgettable love stories.

DESERT LIFE MEDIA

———

Desert Life Media: *There Is Life in The Desert*

Entertainment–first Christian fiction set in the Southwest, featuring redemption, family, and faith

Publishing clean, wholesome, and uplifting fiction since 2010

———

desertlifemedia.com

www.ingramcontent.com/pod-product-compliance
Lightning Source LLC
Chambersburg PA
CBHW051943220626
47052CB00004B/777